THE FALLEN ONE

A FATED WINGS NOVELLA (BOOK 3)

C.R. JANE

Join C.R. Jane's Readers' Group

Stay up to date with C.R. Jane by joining her Facebook readers' group, C.R.'s Fated Realm. Ask questions, get first looks at new books/series, and have fun with other book lovers!

Join C.R.'s Fated Realm

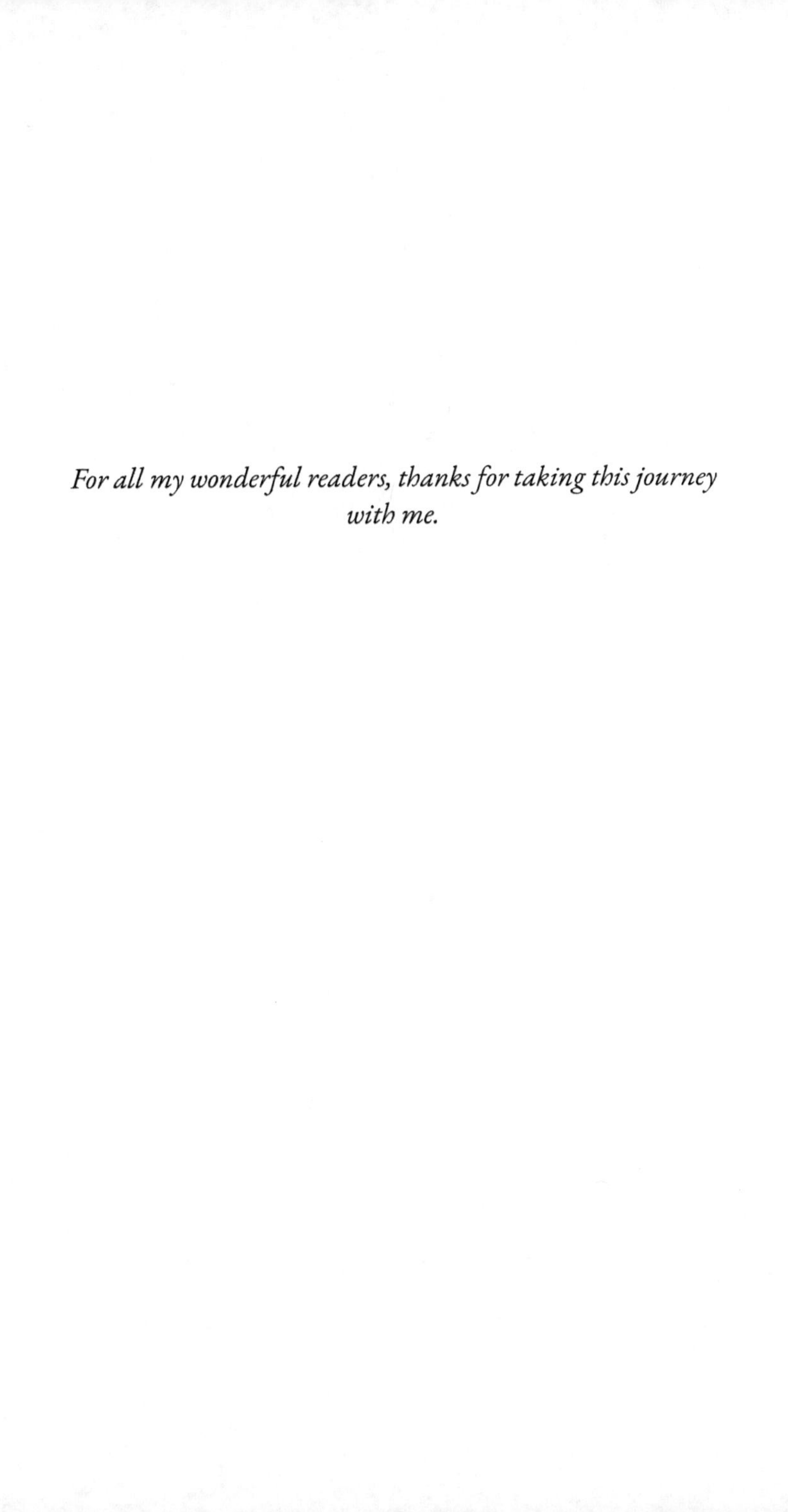

For all my wonderful readers, thanks for taking this journey with me.

The Fated Wings Series

The Fallen One

Damon Pierce.

Football star, devoted lover... arrogant, impulsive fallen angel.

Once a chosen being straight from the heavens, his fall from grace left a mark on his heart that he didn't think could ever be erased.

Discover his story, along with never before published scenes with his obsession, Eva.

The Fallen One is a romantic adventure you won't want to miss.

"He remembered the forceful hand that cast him to the earth. He'd fallen like a shooting star, his flesh burning until his wings fell away. Pain was something he had never known before. But even worse than the physical affliction was the knowledge that he would forevermore be denied Heaven."

—— James Burnham, The Fruit of the Fallen

 PROLOGUE

Now

Two months. Two months of fruitless searching. Two months of wanting to tear my heart out of my chest so I don't have to feel the pain that her disappearance has left in me. I haven't found a clue as to where she went. Had I made her unhappy? Had she chosen to leave me? I can't bear the thought that she left me on purpose, but at the same time the thought that someone has taken her fills me with a dread and rage that seeps out of every pore in my body.

I've searched every inch of the city, and still nothing. I go to take a sip of my drink but find that it's empty. What number am I on? Does it really matter? I hang my head over the balcony and gaze down at the city. My city. The passersby walking on the sidewalk below look tiny to me. I want to bellow and curse at them...throw my glass at them. How dare they go about their everyday lives like my life isn't in shambles.

Maybe I'm doomed to never find true happiness again, and certainly not the happiness that comes from having someone like Eva in your life. My mind wanders to another time, another life, moments that I thought I had finally been able to leave behind thanks to Eva. Moments before...

ONE

If I could die, I would have died from boredom ages ago. I've been trapped on this insufferable planet for what seems like forever now, not long enough to forget how much better Paradise is mind you, but long enough that the days all seem to blur together. Every day is the same, watch the humans, protect the humans, fight the bad guys. It goes on and on, running on repeat until I could probably go about my day blindfolded and still achieve the same results. I remember being so excited about this mission when I first got the call. I'm an idiot. Note to self. Leaving Paradise is never a good idea. There's a reason everyone is trying to get into it.

Angels are born from fire, or at least that's what they tell me. I can't remember anything beyond being the form that I am now. We do not *become* angels, we simply *are* angels. I am one of seven Archangels, the guardian class of the heavens. I'm great at my job, in fact, I'm the fucking best. Now, now, don't get offended by my language. I'm sure when you think of angels you think of harps and cute fat babies with tiny wings. I assure you, I'm no tiny baby...anywhere.

My comrades and I are called Watchers, sent to guard the

human race from the Fallen. As a council, we rule over the lesser angels and direct them with their everyday tasks. I spend my days hovering right outside the fringes of mankind, never actually interacting with the beings I have been sent to protect.

It's funny about humans. They run around constantly, so sure in their own superiority, unaware of the powers that circle around them. They worship Gods that don't exist, and slaughter each other like fools over the pettiest of inconveniences. Everything that they hold dear becomes meaningless once they die.

I resent them. I resent that they are so important to the Creator that I've been tasked to toil away my days protecting them despite the fact that they are complete and utter idiots. I miss Paradise. I miss the sweet smell in the air, the light melody that always seems to be playing nearby. There's no imperfections in Paradise. Everything has its place and purpose. There's no worries...only fun. And the girls...I miss the girls most of all. So fucking gorgeous. So fucking arrogant as well, but with a body like that who needs a soul. I've yet to find a human that even remotely reminds me of them. I'm starved for sex at this point. Don't get me wrong, there's been some nymphs that have kept my attention for a hot second, but overall, I'm deeply dissatisfied with my sex life since I came to this place. Me, I've never wanted a soul. I've never seen the need for it. I'm already perfect. As far as I've seen, having a soul just gives you a lot of complications. All this talk about right and wrong, it's exhausting. For an angel, the only wrong is the Fallen. The rest is just a mix of fighting, eating, fucking, and sleeping some.

Humans are filled with so many...emotions. It's hard to stomach, and the fact that they remind me of leeches doesn't help the situation. How such imperfect creatures got the chance at souls is deeply disturbing to me. My time on this mission should be ending soon though. And then I'm never leaving Paradise again.

Torin, my brother for all intents and purposes, is sprawled out on the grass beside me, whittling away at a piece of wood in the meadow that we've adopted as our own. We've battled by each other's side from the very beginning. There's no one on this pitiful excuse of a world that I trust more.

We're taking a break from our usual schedule. The Fallen have been more active as of late and even I've tired of the constant battles. There's only so much search, fight, and destroy that can happen before you get annoyed. Their activity has been somewhat puzzling though. We always have the usual struggle for whose side the humans are going to be on, but the Fallen have never been known for strategy in their attacks. It's usually a one-on-one kind of thing where a Fallen gets bored and decides to steal a human's soul for fun. The fact that they seem to be traveling in packs now is confusing. Their actions almost seem like they are more focused on keeping us busy, than actually turning a mortal's heart.

Torin is still concentrating on his piece of wood. He saw a human carpenter doing it once and is now determined to master the skill. The only problem with this is that Torin has no artistic talent whatsoever. I'm not sure how an angel has managed to be so imperfect at such a lowly skill, but he's done it. I have a collection on my windowsill of shapeless blobs of wood that Torin has given me. According to Torin, these blobs are supposed to be representative of the female form. According to me, they actually are more representative of a large man's buttocks.

"I think this one is done!" he announces proudly, holding up his chunk of wood.

"Well done," I say absentmindedly, staring up into the cottony clouds, still musing over the Fallen's actions.

"You can add this to your collection," he continues excitedly. He lays the wood beside me. I glance at it briefly before continuing to analyze the Fallen's latest movements. A pebble bounces off my head and I glare at him annoyed. He has light brown hair that sticks up all over the place and there's always a merry twinkle in his bright brown eyes. He reminds me of a puppy I realize as I throw a pebble back at him.

"What's on your mind?" he asks in an amused tone. Torin has always been far more lighthearted than me. I sometimes wonder how we can both be from the warrior class. Torin's heart is never in the mission, always finding things to distract him from his duties, like carving. I spend half of my time just making sure he doesn't get his head cut off since he spends his days with his head in the clouds rather than on our job.

I turn my head to look at him. "Have you noticed anything different in the way the Fallen have been attacking lately?"

"Different?" he laughingly asks. "You mean besides the fact that they smell worse than usual? Nope." He pops his lips as he says "nope" and I roll my eyes in frustration at him. It would be nice if at least some of the time he could take anything seriously. It's difficult to tell between a Fallen and other angels such as myself. We are all ridiculously good looking no matter what side of the aisle we are on. It would be useful if they did carry a stench to differentiate them.

Torin doesn't talk about Paradise very much. He doesn't even seem to mind it here. I have a sneaking suspicion that this is because of the major upgrade in prestige and ranking he received by becoming a Watcher. In Paradise he had been one of the angels that was often overlooked because of his somewhat lazy and easygoing nature, and it was only because of my influence that he ended up as one of the seven Watchers in the first place. When I first got the assignment from the Seraph Leadership, I was ecstatic at the opportunity. I had reached the point where the only way up the ranks was to start fighting the

Seraph Leadership for their spots. I saw a position as head of the Watcher council as a way to delay that for a while. Plus, one of my regulars had gotten a bit needy, and there was only so much of her cock blocking me at every turn that I could take.

Torin had been miserable at the prospect of being left behind and had begged me to find a way for him to come along. Angels with Torin's temperament usually found themselves either as a member of one of the Seraph's courts or as a trainer of weaker Archangels. Torin may have been easygoing and lazy, but he lusted over power. In the back of my mind I always wondered if we would have been such close friends if I wasn't who I was.

If I was honest with myself, Torin brought down the whole counsel. It was supposed to be a group of the most talented and capable of the Creator's warriors. Torin definitely didn't fit that bill. I couldn't remember a time when he wasn't in my life though, and I did my best to help him overcome his many shortcomings even if it made my life harder.

Shaking myself from my reverie, I sit up and brush grass off my shirt. "We should probably get going," I tell him, standing up and letting my wings surge out, the feathers moving slightly in the breeze. I may be an arrogant bastard, but my wings are fucking impressive. Charcoal black with strands of silver, and with a wingspan longer than my frame, they stand out, even among the other Watchers. Even now, with as many times as Torin has seen my wings, he stares at them longingly, a bit of jealousy seeping out of his eyes.

"I can't go today," Torin says, shifting his weight uneasily.

"Why not?" I ask him confused. What else would he have to do during the day then fight Fallen?

"Jarbin has asked me to help him. There's some sort of nest of Fallen over near Arondale that he wants me to help clean out."

"Do I need to go with you?" I ask. It's very strange that Jarbin would ask Torin of all people to help him out. His teammate, Marco, is perfectly capable of helping him clean out a nest. Jarbin knows that Torin is more of a liability on a mission like that. As a council, we had recently made it a policy that we should always hunt in pairs. The rise in Fallen activity had put more than one council member in dangerous situations that they almost didn't get out of. I had always taken Torin hunting with me anyway to protect his skin, so the policy hadn't been that big of a change for me. For Jarbin to ask Torin to accompany him right after we put the policy in place was annoying.

Torin must have seen the suspicion on my face. "Jarbin knows that you've been covering for me a lot lately. He just thinks it would be a good way for me to get more practice in and give you a break." Again, this doesn't sound like Jarbin but if he wants to take over responsibility for not getting Torin killed, a break sounds kind of nice.

"You don't really need a partner most of the time anyway," he laughs at me. This is true. Basically, the only reason I even like having a partner is that I have someone to talk to when I'm waiting for a Fallen to appear.

My wings flutter, and I can feel the faint itch under my skin that signals it's time to start. One thing about me, I can't sit still for very long. There's nothing that compares to the rush of adrenaline of fighting and even though I complain about how active the Fallen have been lately, I know secretly its satisfying that bloodlust I keep deep inside of me.

"Well, don't die hunting with Jarbin," I tell Torin shortly, preparing to leave. Torin stands up and clasps my shoulder, a strange glimmer in his eye that's hard to read.

"Stay safe out there my brother," he tells me.

"Always," I say cockily, pushing off from the ground and taking flight. There's an uneasy tingling along my spine as I soar away though, looking back once and finding Torin staring out after me, a small smile on his face that's so different from the grin he usually throws out. I shake the feeling off and concentrate on the task ahead, my mind already thinking of new fighting moves to use against the Fallen today. Battling by myself will be a rare treat.

Two

I'm soaring, the breeze brushes against my cheek as I go in and out of the cloud line, watching the ground half-heartedly for signs of anything amiss. I'm actually enjoying the solitude. I've realized that Torin is quite the chatter box. Having someone to talk to is a bit overrated when you're hunting hidden Fallen.

A flash of light catches my eye in some trees below. I change direction rapidly, speeding down to check it out. I land on the ground, looking around for anything amiss. I'm in a forest clearing, tall pines stand proudly around me. The light dances through the trees, hitting puddles that are strewn all over the ground from the recent rainfall. I wonder if I just saw the light reflecting off of one of those. Shadows dance between the trees, catching my attention. The air is quiet, too quiet, which is why I feel like something is amiss. An anxious feeling passes over me. There aren't even birds chirping. That never happens in a forest this dense. I retract my wings back into my body, and crouch down to look at a red stain in the grass. The red liquid comes off on my fingers, I put my hand to my nose to smell it and immediately the iron tang of blood hits my senses. Maybe an animal has been injured?

Right as I stand up to see if there is any more blood, something hits my side with the force of what feels like a thousand boulders. I smash into a tree. It gives a large shudder before crashing to the ground in a thunderous clatter. Before I can regain my wits, I'm pulled up and thrown again to the other side of the clearing. I roll my body and just miss impaling myself on a long tree branch. I thrust my body up in the air, regaining my feet just before I feel the sharp sting of a sword nick the side of my ribcage. I roar in rage and finally make eye contact with my unknown assailant. Of course, it's one of the Fallen. He's so pale I wonder if he has some sort of condition. A shock of red hair is pulled back in a long braid behind him. He's wearing a look of hatred so fierce it gives me pause for a moment, wondering how someone could hate a perfect stranger so much.

Someone approaches me from behind at the same time the pale Fallen comes at me again from the front with his long broadsword. I bring an elbow sharply behind me, hearing a satisfying crack as my elbow meets something that was obviously important to the creep behind me. I catch the tip of the sword in between my hands, a nifty trick that has taken hundreds of years to perfect. The Fallen gives me a look of shock as I twist the sword out of his hands and flip it into the air. Grabbing it fluidly, I swipe the blade swiftly across his neck. A sick slicing sound fills the air as the red head's body stays suspended in the air for a moment before thumping to the ground, his head rolling off.

I only have a moment to relish his death before the other Fallen is once again attacking me from behind. Arms are thrown around my throat, the pressure feels like a steel vice is crushing my windpipe. A crash through the trees signals that others are coming. Bending my weight down, I use the momentum to flip the assailant's body over mine. He winces as he hits the ground hard, his head bouncing a few times and momentarily striking him still. I still have the broadsword in my hand and I take advantage of his confusion to thrust the blade deep in his chest. He gasps for breath and blood begins to trickle from his mouth.

Satisfied that he is down for the count I crouch into a fighting position to prepare for the others. Two more Fallen approach me at the same time. I pick up a decomposing log from off the ground and swing it around, hitting both of them at the same time and sending them flying.

More Fallen begin to emerge from the trees, so many that they resemble ants swarming from a nest that has been disturbed. I yank the sword from out of the Fallen's heart and begin swinging. The air is thick with the scent of blood, sweat, and screams. I can taste the rage of the Fallen in the air as they attack without mercy. As soon as I cut one down, another takes its place. My body is littered with gouges so deep that the blood is making it difficult to hold onto the sword because it's so slippery. My left eye is swollen shut, and the right one isn't much better. I'm having to use all of my other senses just to stay standing.

Finally, I acknowledge this is a battle that I can't win by myself and I prepare to take flight. My wings shoot out creating a sudden burst of wind so strong that it knocks over at least five of the Fallen in front of me. I rise a few inches off the ground before crashing back down to the ground as several Fallen hit me from above. They swarm out of the trees, continuing to land on top of me until the weight is so great that I can't breathe. My wings are pulled, feathers are ripped out ferociously, and sharp swords make long diagonal tears so deep that I imagine you could see through them if you tried. My wings rendered useless, I focus all of my energy on pulling myself out of the pile which is now made up of so many Fallen that I imagine they have no idea where I actually am beneath them.

Using anything at my disposal, including my teeth and nails, I drag myself from under the pile into the thick underbrush of the forest. I take a glance back and see that there must be at least twenty Fallen wrestling on the pile. No one seems to notice that I've managed to crawl my way out. My breath comes in sharp gasps. It feels like at least one of my lungs has been punctured. Sharp twigs and rocks get stuck in the feathers of my wings, grinding against the cuts and bruises, causing agonizing pain. I crawl for hours until I can no longer hear the yells of my attackers. Just when I don't think I can go on for any longer, I see a large opening in a cliff that is just big enough for me to squeeze in. Sending a silent prayer up to the heavens that there aren't any predators slumbering within, I squeeze my body into the crevice. The effort takes the last of my energy and I immediately faint from a combination of exhaustion and blood loss.

Three

After

The gorgeous creature is staring up at me, a look of awe and recognition on her face. Eva. It's the perfect name for her. Across most cultures it means "life" or "living one," and looking at her I feel like I've finally come alive for the first time. She looks away from me and I feel immediately bereft. In that moment I know that I would do anything to keep those amethyst eyes looking at me forever.

Every guy who was in the immediate area is flocked around her, each trying to catch her attention and see if she is alright. She's blushing, and I instantly fall a little in love at the idea of this goddess being embarrassed by so much attention. She's easily the most perfect being I've ever seen. No way in hell would most girls react that way. She's had to have gotten nonstop adoration her entire life and I wonder at how she could have such a reaction still.

She's deliberately ignoring me, talking to douche bag Eric who's soaking up her attention. Why she's chosen to give the little weasel her attention is beyond me. I glare at some of the guys crowded around us and they back up a little bit. Such is her appeal that even I, the god of this school, can't make them totally leave the scene. Eric smooths some of her hair behind her ears and I feel the sudden urge to rip off his head, or at least cut off the offending hand.

Her voice makes her even more attractive if that's possible. It's low and throaty, and so sensual that I'm hard at the very sound of it. She says she's fine, but the tense set of her shoulders tell a different story. I want to believe that she can feel the weight of the attraction between us, but it seems like that idea is just wishful thinking since she hasn't spared me a glance since that first fateful look.

Eric continues to ask her questions and touch her, finally asking her to go to the movies with him. I've had enough. I finally regain the use of my tongue and say something before he can whisk her away. "Aren't you going to introduce me to your friend?" I ask Eric, pretending like I'm being solicitous towards him. I can tell Eric was just waiting for me to pounce. The skin around his mouth is pursed from the effort it is taking not to show how annoyed he is with me. But seriously dude, when did the concept of "dibs" ever really work.

"Of course," he tells me, introducing me to Eva. Her hesitance is tangible and I wonder what I've done wrong already for her to want nothing to do with me. I hold out my hand to her, wanting to touch this girl's skin so bad that I fear I might just start crying if she rejects me. Her eyes hold me captive again once they finally meet mine. She uncertainly touches my hand and immediately I feel like I've found my home for the first time since I left Paradise. Unable to stop myself, I brush my lips against her hand. I can feel her begin to tremble at my touch and my heart skips a beat. That must mean that I'm making her feel something right? Or, it means that I'm disgusting her and she's shaking because she wants me to stop holding her hand. I choose to ignore that possibility and enjoy the sparks that are going up and down my arm from where we are touching. My lips are slightly tingling from where they touched her skin. I've never come close to having this reaction to someone before. Every girl I've ever been with fades from memory.

"It's a pleasure Eva," I tell her with a wink. "I'm sorry that this idiot decided he couldn't throw the ball today. But I'm not sorry that it led me to meeting you."

I immediately want to punch myself. That was the best that I could come up with? She pulls her hand away and I don't blame her. I'm sure she has seen some smooth lines in her lifetime and those definitely fell short. I'm a fucking idiot. They turn to walk away, and I feel desperate.

"What movie are you going to?" I ask quickly. Eric is close to attacking me I can tell. It's taking everything in him to keep his cool. He's always been a fucking hothead. He will be too easy to rile up in this situation, especially since the stakes up for grabs are Eva.

"Not sure yet, but we have to go if we are going to fit it in before practice," he tells me, gritting his teeth with a look that is clearly telling me to fuck off.

Eva is looking at me intently now, and I can't help but hope that the glimmer in her gaze is a little hope that I'll come to the movie with them. "Why don't the rest of us come along?" I tell Eric, gesturing to the besotted fools still hovering around us. I've backed Eric into a corner bringing in the rest of the guys. Although he should have a problem saying no to me as his Team Captain, Eric has never had a problem showing how much he hates my guts. By mentioning the rest of the guys though, I forced his hand. He would look like a huge prick if he said no to the rest of his teammates. Eric reluctantly nods, right on the edge of his breaking point. His grip on Eva tightening a little too much for my comfort. I want to break every one of his fingers when I see the uncomfortableness in Eva's expression. I'm about to step in when she surprises me by slowly breaking his grip and taking a step away from him. Her actions clearly illustrate "this guy is not my boyfriend," and I'm beyond pleased at her actions. Maybe I do have a chance.

I watch Eva as we walk to the theater that is just down the block. Her perfect ass sways innocently. She's not trying to entice anyone, she just exudes a sexuality so strong that it's taking everything in me to keep my dick down. A quick glance at the others around me confirms that they can't keep their eyes off her ass either. Let's be honest though, the whole package is fucking appealing as hell. Her legs are killer, and I can't help but imagine what it would feel like if they were wrapped around me.

We get to the theater sooner than I would like since it means I have to actually pay attention to things like paying for tickets instead of staring at Eva. She's looking around the theater with a little bit of awe and I'm perplexed. This movie theater is definitely not one of the nicer ones I have been to. She's looking at it like it's Disneyland though. While the others discuss what we should see, she wanders off towards the concession stand. I immediately take the opportunity to go after her before anyone else does.

Eva is standing in front of the concession check out, gazing in wonder at all of the choices. I stare in amusement at her. She's acting like she's never seen a Kit Kat before… although with a body like that, maybe she hasn't. I step up behind her. "What do you want to get?" I ask. She doesn't turn around and doesn't seem shocked that I'm right behind her.

"The biggest tub of popcorn they sell," she replies laughingly.

Maybe I was wrong about her being one of those girls that doesn't eat. "A girl after my own heart," I tell her. She says she wants a soda too, so I turn to order our food, looking at the checkout person for the first time. Oh boy, I inwardly roll my eyes. It's a young girl who looks like her tongue is about to fall out of her mouth due to how much she is drooling. I flash her a grin and her eyes roll back a bit. Fuck, I hope she doesn't faint. I hate when they do that. It also clashes with the whole approachable vibe I'm trying to give Eva.

"Could we please have your XL tub of popcorn, extra butter, two Cokes, and..." I turn to ask Eva what candy she wants.

"I can pay for myself," she answers adorably, but it makes me wonder. Is she really this sweet, or is this an act? I've never met a girl who actually meant they would pay for themselves if I offered. Something about her strikes me as authentic though. There's no calculating gleam in her beautiful eyes. I look at what she's wearing for the first time. I can tell that it came from somewhere cheap, definitely a far cry from the designer duds of the girls I usually hook up with. She looks far better in her cheap clothes than they ever did in their thousand-dollar outfits though.

"What candy do you want?" I ask again. I grin when she tells me Sour Patch Kids, it's one of my favorites as well. I finish placing my order and grimace when the concession girl squeaks out a request for my autograph. This kind of situation is basically a lose-lose for me. I either respond no to the girl and come off looking like a jerk to both the girl and Eva, or I say yes, and Eva thinks I'm a self-important prick. I choose to give the autograph and tense when I look back at Eva after I've finished and picked up the food. She's staring at the gigantic movie posters on the wall though, looking again like a little child seeing Disneyland for the first time. If she has this reaction to a shitty movie theater, maybe I should take her to Disneyland. She would love me forever. We walk over to the rest of the group and Eric stalks over.

"Eva, why didn't you wait for me?" he asks her.

I roll my eyes at his indignation and step in front of Eva, a protective streak that I don't usually have nowadays rising up within me. "Relax man, I paid for her," I tell him sternly, giving him a "hey asshole, chill out" look at the same time.

Eva steps around me, brushing my arm as she passes by and sending chills up and down my body.

"What movie did everyone pick?" she sweetly asks. Everyone tries to answer her at once and Eric reaches out and grabs her hand, pulling her towards him. He's back on my kill list with that move and I grit my teeth in an effort not to pull him away from her and throw him through the glass entrance doors. She once again pulls away from him to walk towards the ticket stand, my stomach doing internal cheers at the fact that they clearly aren't a thing. Not that them being a thing would stop me at all. She again tries to pay for her ticket much to the displeasure of all of the guys and I'm again falling for her sweetness.

We walk into the theater where Captain America is playing, and I give my teammates my best alpha male glance to make sure I get to sit next to her. I pass her the popcorn bucket and get embarrassingly aroused watching her eat. She savors each bite like the cheap butter popcorn is the best thing she has ever eaten. She gives a little moan at the end of her first few bites that immediately drags my mind to how I could make her moan louder than that. The movie starts and again her excitement is contagious. She's leaning forward in her seat, so enthralled with the characters on the screen that it's contagious and all of a sudden, the movie becomes the best movie I've ever seen as well. She has so much excitement for such a small thing. It makes me try to remember when the last time I got even half as excited about anything. It's been forever. Even sex has taken on a humdrum feeling. Looking her over in the dim lighting, the movie reflecting in those gorgeous eyes, I'm pretty positive that sex with her wouldn't be same old same old. My dick tightens more just thinking about it. I'm a little disgusted at my inability to control myself but looking around I see that every guy around is staring at her and most likely feeling the same way.

Eric tries to move in at some point, putting his hand right above her knee. I give a little snort when she scoots closer to me, moving away from him awkwardly and leaving a very disappointed look on his face. The asshole. I make sure to keep her well-fed for the rest of the movie thinking at least I have that going for me that I can give her treats. She's sitting really close to me and I want to pick up the armrest so we can get even closer. I doubt she's ready for that though after the four words we've spoken to each other. I tell her a few jokes that Beckham told me the other day and am rewarded with a laugh that's as sexy as the rest of her. It shoots straight down to my balls and I want to keep her laughing for the rest of her life. I'm the least smooth I've ever been but it seems to be working at least a little bit. She's definitely not an open book and I'm constantly studying everything about her to try and see what she's thinking.

The movie goes by much quicker than I would like. My stomach sinks at the thought of having to go to practice and not being able to see her. What if she doesn't want to see me again? I watch her as I walk. She's talking to one of the guys about the movie, a cute pep in her step. I feel like a love-sick fool getting so obsessed over everything she does, but I can't help it. One of the guys asks me about some of the actors in the movie and I tell them they're nice guys. I've acted with a few of them from the last movie I dabbled in last summer, and Beckham's acted with the rest of them in a couple of films. I notice Eva's listening to our conversation interestedly and I wonder what she thinks of Beckham. There aren't a lot of girls who aren't obsessed with one of our trio and I just have to hope that she's more partial to tall, dark, and handsome, rather than sun god blonde.

Both Beckham and Mason would go crazy over her even with them being as big, if not bigger, manwhores than me. A wave of possessiveness washes over me at the thought of them seeing her. Unfortunately, I live with Mason. If I get to the point where she's coming over, and I'm going to do whatever I can to make that happen, I'm going to have to find a way that they aren't there at the same time. Realizing I'm getting way ahead of myself I go back to watching Eva's seductive walk all the way back to campus.

Once we get to campus I give a big 'fuck off' to all of my teammates, including Eric. He doesn't get the hint though, not wanting to give up whatever claim he has over Eva due to the unfortunate fact he must have met her first or something. I'm glaring so hard at Eric that I almost miss Eva scurrying away. Eric runs after her and gets her to agree to go to breakfast with him. I'm already plotting to make sure that breakfast doesn't happen. He pulls her into a long hug and kisses the top of her head. I finally have had enough and walk towards him aggressively. He must get the message because he gives me a smirk and walks away. I already know practice is going to be painful for him as I'm going to make sure he gets tackled hard whatever chance I can get.

She's walking away from me again and I start to panic. "Eva, wait," I call after her. It takes her a moment to turn around and when she does I immediately want to wrap her in my arms. She has a forlorn look on her face like everything is hopeless. I want to tell her that I know what hopeless is, and she's the opposite of that.

"I would like to see you again, preferably as soon as possible," I tell her, giving her my most charming smile.

"I'm not sure that's a good idea," she tells me hesitantly, a sucker punch that I wasn't expecting.

"Why?" I ask, dumbfounded that she would say yes to asshole Eric but no to me.

"Well, you're Damon Pierce. And I don't think that you would be good for me," she replies.

Her answer makes perfect sense to me. It is few and far between when I'm good for anyone. For her I could be good though, I could be oh so good. And for once I mean it. I would do anything to get a chance with this girl.

"You're oblivious, aren't you?" I answer. "I should be thinking the same thing. I don't think there's a guy on this planet who would be good enough for you Eva Taylor."

Her face is soft as if my words are melting whatever barrier she has erected around her heart. "Just give me a chance," I beg her softly.

I feel like I've been stabbed when she shakes her head and hurries inside her dorm, taking a piece of me with her. My hands are shaking a little. I feel like a junkie who is already in withdrawal thinking about how I haven't secured seeing her again.

I hustle to practice. My mind is whirling so much that I actually have to concentrate a little to get through practice. I'm so upset I don't even have it in me to cheer when Eric gets manhandled on a play and ends up having to sit on the sideline because he's hurt.

I can't help walking by her dorm on the way home. Eva's got me in knots. I have to see her again.

Four

I wake with a start from my blood loss induced rest. I'm pretty confident now that I'm going to die since my immortal body has yet to start healing itself. My whole body feels like it's been ripped into pieces. My wings give a soft flutter beneath me. I'm laying on them, I can feel that both of them have been broken in several places. I'm frankly surprised that the Fallen didn't manage to just rip them off of me and finish me that way. An angel can't live without its wings after all. I suppose they thought it would be better if I died slowly, in this mind-altering pain, than dying suddenly. I've never felt such agony. I feel absurdly happy to still have my wings though.

I take a deep, shuddery breath. Even breathing requires concentration. It's like my body has already decided that it's done. I lay still for a moment, just focusing on the air going in and out of my body. I need to drag myself out of this cave just in case the pack of Fallen comes by to make sure I've been finished off. I'll just rest for one second and then I can start to move.

Time ticks by slowly. I'm aware of every sound around me,

just waiting for one of the Fallen to appear. Finally, when I feel like breathing isn't taking as much of an effort, I attempt to pull myself from the tiny cave. After what seems like an hour I manage to pull myself out. I immediately collapse to the ground, trembling with the pain that has doubled with that small effort. I check 'walking' off my mental list of things I'm capable of doing and decide that I'm just going to have to keep dragging myself. Eventually Torin or one of my other brothers will come looking for me. Right?

Inch by inch I pull myself through the thick underbrush, every small movement feeling like someone is driving nails into every portion of my body. Just a little bit further I tell myself. Sweat is pouring off my body, the smallest exertion even too much for my perfected form. I have to take breaks frequently, my body unable to handle the strain. I've never felt so helpless.

This goes on for hours. I know that I have barely made any headway. Every rustle of leaves has me bracing for a Fallen's face to pop out from behind a tree. I hear the trickle of water off in the distance. Suddenly I'm painfully aware of how dry my throat is and how much I have been sweating over the last few hours. With a destination in mind I set off, inch by excruciating inch.

I'm so intent on just surviving that I fail to see the portions of the underbrush that are hiding a steep ravine until the ground gives way beneath me and I find myself bouncing down the side of a steep cliff where the river I heard earlier churns angrily beneath me.

I fall into the water, immediately sinking to the bottom quickly as my fatigue and wounds make it impossible for me to rise above the surface. My wings feel like they are actually made of stone and they contribute to pulling me down into the swirling black depths of the river.

"Immortal my ass," I think to myself bitterly as my consciousness fades to black.

....

I wake up to a cold cloth patting my face. I rush to sit up and then collapse with a groan. I'm definitely still significantly injured...but I'm alive, which is more than I could have hoped for. I slowly regain use of my faculties. My body still hurts everywhere I can say for certain, but the extent of my remaining injuries is unclear. It does seem that my healing powers have begun to kick in though. I begin evaluating my body, trying to move my wings at least a little when the cold cloth descends onto my face again. The room finally comes into focus and I find myself staring up at a nervous, frail looking human girl.

At first glance she is homely, little more than skin and bones. She's dressed in what looks like a pile of rags and there's a smudge of dirt on her slightly too large nose. We stare at each other, each analyzing the other. Her hand is frozen in the air holding the dripping rag that she had been patting my face with. Immediately realizing she isn't a threat, I ignore her and begin to survey my surroundings.

I'm in a small structure, more hut than house, that has seen better days. The floor is made up of a packed red clay that's cracked and broken in places. The walls of the structure look like they are nothing but sticks bound together with sinew or something similar. There's a rough door made of a few planks of wood and some animal skin covering the entrance to the structure and little holes have been left open in the walls, either by design, or by decay. A slight breeze flows through them carrying with it the slight iron scent of blood from an animal that must have been slaughtered nearby recently. It's basically a shit hole.

The girl makes a small coughing noise. I turn to look at her and raise an eyebrow. She's fiddling with the rag and staring at my large wings that stretch almost the entire shack. "Youuuuu have wings," she stutters out.

I roll my eyes and wince as even that movement sends pain thundering through my head. "Smart one aren't you?" I ask sarcastically.

Her brow furrows at my words. I continue to ignore her as I assess if I'm going to be able to drag myself out of the structure on my own volition. Thinking about dragging myself out of the place reminds me of the fact that this girl is literally half my size. Which obviously begs the question...how the hell did I get out of the river.

I turn to look at her. She's still staring at me with a mix of awe and a little fear, her brow still furrowed. "You're a particularly tiny human," I say to her.

She gives me a look that clearly states that now she thinks I'm the idiot. "You're being awfully rude considering I saved your life you know," she tells me. Her voice is rough and frankly, slightly hard on my ears. I'm impressed with the little sass in her speech though. I wouldn't have thought such a mouse would be capable of that.

I roll my eyes at her. "Little human, I'm obviously talking about the fact that I'm sure I outweigh you by at least a hundred pounds. How the fuck did you get me out of that river?" I ask. She looks proud of herself now.

"I'm not telling you until you say thank you. Even beings such as yourself...whatever you are, should know how to say thank you."

I stare at her in disbelief. "Thank you?" I tell her, the words sounding foreign on my tongue.

"Yes, good job. Although the way you say it seems like it's the first time the words have crossed your lips," she tells me.

I'm flabbergasted at the audacity of this little urchin girl, and I feel a small flush hit my cheeks that a human would talk to me this way.

She walks to a trunk that is pushed against the wall of the house. From out of the trunk, she pulls a rope that looks like it has been doused in something. She brings it over to me, drops it at my feet, and puts her hands on her hips proudly. "Now what do you think of that?" she says.

I look at her dully. "I have no idea what this has to do with you saving me," I tell her haughtily.

"Well that's how I saved you," she sputters. "The water wasn't deep. You were just so broken up that you sank to the bottom. I was washing some clothes in the river when I saw you roll down that hill. It was just a matter of stepping into the water to put the rope around you. I tied the end of the rope to my horse and there you go," she explains.

I notice for the first time that her clothes are wet up to her relatively flat chest. She's so short that I realize she must have been right. There were no "murky depths," my body simply gave out. I'm mildly impressed, but also mildly embarrassed that this human had to save me.

"Well good job for showing more ingenuity than your kind is usually known for," I tell her, enjoying the angry sparkle in her eyes at my comment. She says nothing and begins to grab some white cloths from another trunk. She approaches me without asking permission and begins to wrap some of my larger wounds with the cloths, spreading a strange smelling poultice on the wounds beforehand. I can tell that she is trying to pull the bandages tighter than they need to be in her annoyance and I laugh at this tiny human trying to hurt me.

"What are you laughing at?" she snaps at me.

"Nothing," I reply innocently, deciding perhaps a little too late that I shouldn't antagonize the person who saved my life too much. She moves to my wings and they give a flutter at her soft touch. "Whoa there," I tell her, not wanting to get aroused in this situation. It's not that she is making me aroused, but my wings have a mind of their own. Sometimes they're basically like having an extension of my dick.

She turns a dark, beet red like she can read my mind and retracts her hands from my wings. "Where else hurts?" she asks.

I carefully continue to evaluate my injuries and am surprised to find that the poultice seems to be speeding up my already remarkable healing power. "What's in this stuff?" I ask, grabbing the poultice away from her and sniffing the contents further to see if I can unmask the ingredients.

"It's my mum's secret recipe," she replies. "We've always been healers in our family."

"Where's your family now?" I ask, looking around suspiciously like they are going to come in from the front entry flap any time now. That's the last thing I need is more humans getting a good luck at my wings since they are still too injured to be able to retract.

A shuttered look passes over her face. "They're gone," she says in a pain filled voice that speaks volumes. I generally have very little sympathy for the human race, but the thought of this tiny girl being alone feels wrong to me.

"Is it just you here then?" I ask tentatively. She gives a quiet nod and begins pulling more things out of her trunk. I'm wondering if she's actually a witch or something and has enchanted the trunks since they seem to hold far more than normal human furniture. I'm distracted from my train of thought when she brings over a chunk of bread with a liberal amount of creamy cheese spread on top. Suddenly I realize I'm famished. I scarf it down so fast that she doesn't have time to move. She's gawking at me like a cow in a field.

"How would you like me to act after not eating for days and being on the verge of death?" I ask her annoyed. She wisely says nothing and cuts me another portion of bread and cheese, this one much larger than the first. I scarf this one down nearly as fast and start to feel a little relief from my hunger, although I'm sure I could still eat an entire beast at the moment if the opportunity presented itself. She pours some water from a clay pitcher and hands it to me, immediately refilling it when I hand it back to her empty two seconds later.

"So now what?" she asks after I have drunk her entire pitcher.

"What do you mean?"

"Well you obviously can't leave here in your condition. I'm just wondering when you're going to tell me how wonderful I am and ask to stay the night."

This makes me grin. I'm starting to like the little cheek this human is giving me. Not even any angels really dare to talk back to me. "I'm staying the night," I tell her, ignoring her first request. My healing capabilities should have me close to as good as new by morning since they have finally started working. I've already been gone for at least two days by my calculations, and I'm sure the council has started sending out search parties.

"That wasn't what I had in mind, but I'll let it slide," she tells me as she hands me a potato sack filled with cotton to use as a pillow and a threadbare blanket. I look at her "mattress" lying on the floor, it doesn't look much better. I think longingly of my opulent bed in the palace that the council stays in. One thing about humans, they are so far behind in technology and luxury. This girl is living in squalor when it shouldn't take a genius to come up with a better version of a bed. I say nothing though, not because I'm scared to insult her but because we are strictly forbidden from advancing human technology. I'm not even supposed to be talking to this girl but I'm thinking there's probably a loophole in my Watcher contract somewhere that covers when a human girl saves you...because I'm sure that was contemplated.

I settle against my potato sack, my wings cushioning my back a little. She blows out the two candles she had burning. I hear some rustling as she changes clothes and I smirk knowing that her face is probably tomato red at the idea of changing in front of me. I hear her lay down on her mattress after a moment. We're both quiet, listening to the sounds of the night. Despite the fact that I'm sure a Fallen wouldn't think to follow me to this place (it's a well-known fact that all angels prefer splendor to squalor), I still keep one ear alert for any sounds that are out of the ordinary. The last thing I want is for a Fallen to discover this place. I feel oddly protective of this odd little creature. Thinking about it, it's actually quite remarkable that she would save something that was clearly not human.

"So what are you?" she squeaks out in the darkness.

"A bird," I respond dryly. I'm unaware of creatures besides angels that would have my type of wings. There might be some fae perhaps, but they are the stuff of legend at this point.

"Haha," she responds in an annoyed voice. "Will you tell me if I guess?"

"How about this, if you can't get it in three guesses than you're too stupid to know." She's quiet for so long that I think she's fallen asleep.

"An angel?" she finally says hesitantly.

"Very good." There's another long pause.

"Does that mean that heaven is real?" she asks, catching me off guard. I hesitate to answer the question, part of what allows a human to have a chance at heaven is the fact that they have to rely on faith to get there. It's something I've always thought a bit unfair, but maybe the tradeoff of having a soul makes it worth it.

"Do you believe in heaven?" I ask her, throwing the question back at her.

"I want to. I want to believe my whole family is up there looking down at me."

Suddenly wanting to comfort this girl I give her the best answer I can without directly telling her Paradise exists and that I've been there. "I'm sure that your family is watching you and missing you just as much as you are missing them." I can almost hear her smile in the darkness and the soft sounds of her snoring a few moments later let me know I succeeded in giving her the answer she was looking for.

It takes me a bit longer to fall asleep despite the fact that my healing body is begging for it. My mind is whirling over the attack and who was behind it. Finally, my body offers me no choice but to fall into a deep slumber. A nagging thought stays right outside of my consciousness as I fall asleep.

FIVE

I wake up far sooner than I would like, the boisterous cawing of birds outside rousing me from a slumber filled with dreams of a beautiful face. I look over at the mattress nearby and see that the human is still sleeping. Camilla. I roll the name over my tongue thinking that the least I could do is try and call her by her name since she did save my life. Deciding to be nicer this morning, I begin examining my body to see how I've healed.

I peel back the bandages that Camilla wrapped around my nastier cuts. I'm surprised that the skin looks good as new, as if nothing happened. That poultice must be magic since even with my supersonic healing I would at least still have a scar for a few days before it disappeared. The rest of my injuries that were under the bandages also look perfect. Examining my arms, chest, and legs, I note that the skin that didn't get the poultice is still a little bruised. I'm going to have to get some to take with me.

Grimacing at the thought of the next step, I tentatively begin to move my wings. They're sore, but so much better than the day before. I send up another silent prayer of thanks that they weren't ripped off my body. I retract them with a loud crack that wakes Camilla from what looked like a deep slumber. I would feel a bit bad, but I need to leave soon and I strangely didn't want to slip out without saying goodbye...and perhaps thank you.

She looks...cute. Her clothes and hair are rumpled and there's a little bit of drool on the side of her mouth. I've never seen a human after they have first woken up and I stare at her in fascination. She notices me staring at her and pats down her hair self-consciously.

"What are you looking at?" she says with a blush, her eyes roving over my bare chest almost hungrily. I let her look, getting to see an angel with minimal clothes, especially one as supremely handsome as myself should be as good as a thank you from my perspective.

"I'd like some of that poultice," I tell her, getting straight to the point. I'm eager to get back to the counsel now that I've healed, and report all that has happened.

"You're leaving already?" she says worriedly. "But aren't you still too injured?"

I hold out my arms to show her that they look almost as good as new. She's gaping again. I'm sure that although the poultice seems to help speed up healing, she's never seen its healing powers combined with angelic healing power.

She stands up and brushes down her dress. "Do you want to at least stay for breakfast?" she asks, walking back over to those magic trunks to pull out some food. I'm more than starving after the meager bread and cheese meal from the night before and I again hungrily scarf down the same meal. I wonder if she eats this all the time, it would certainly explain the fact that she's basically nothing more than skin and bones.

She's left one of the trunks open and when I stand up after eating, a flash of color catches my eye. I walk over and peruse through the trunk before she can say anything. Spying a piece of parchment that has a shock of color on it, I pull it out of the trunk and unroll it so that I can see the whole thing. Much to my surprise...it's spectacular.

She's painted a sunset, but it's unlike any other human artwork I have ever seen. The sky is awash with colors so vibrant that they leap off the page. It's so beautiful that it reminds me of the sunsets in Paradise. She has somehow managed to perfectly replicate the exact color of a fading sun. I'm in awe as I silently feast on the magnificence of the picture.

"It's terrible I know," comes a shaking voice from behind me. I turn to gape at the little human who has just blown my mind with her talent.

"I hope you don't actually believe that," I tell her seriously. "This rivals any artwork I have ever seen, and I have seen all the greats," I tell her. That deep red flush is present in her cheeks as her eyes fill with hope.

"You really think so?" she asks.

I ignore her question and begin to rifle through the trunk, trying to see if there is any other buried treasure within its depths. Much to my delight I find several more parchment papers filled with paintings even better than the first. There's a self-portrait that she must have done while standing in front of a mirror. She has somehow perfectly captured the insecurity and loneliness so present in her eyes and I like that she painted herself as she really looked, imperfections and all. There's another of a river that I have a sneaking suspicion is the one that she saved me from. I give an involuntary shudder as I think about the fact that I almost drowned. I've never really feared death in all of the battles I have fought since I've always had no doubt about my physical prowess. This experience has shaken me however. Angels may be immortal, but we also have no soul. Which means if I did die, I would cease to exist. I shudder one more time and then push it out of my mind, examining Camilla's amazing creations closer.

"I'm going to take this one," I announce, rolling up the picture of the sunset.

"You really want that?" she asks in amazement.

I nod, and then walk out her door so that I can return and report to the council, I've delayed long enough.

"Wait!" she calls out breathlessly, running out from her shanty, holding a jar of the poultice.

I'm once again struck by this human's generosity and the idea of never seeing her again strikes my heart. I have very few true friends in this life, much less ones who would save my life let alone a stranger's life. Maybe it wouldn't be so bad if I secretly visited her.

I take the jar and hold out my hand, unsure what the human custom is for saying goodbye to someone who saved your life.

"Will I see you again?" she asks mournfully, the loneliness seeping out of her.

I internally debate what to say. If the rest of the council finds out, there will be hell to pay. But I don't see why I can't have friendship with Camilla. The main goal behind the policy is to prevent us from fucking humans so we don't create any half angel/half human monsters. But that's easy enough to control since angels choose when they reproduce. Plus, there's not an ounce of me that wants to go there with Camilla. She's more like...what I imagine a little sister feels like. Not that angels have little sisters, but I'm sure I can imagine it.

"I don't know when I'll be back, but I'll stop by with some new painting supplies sometime soon," I tell her. Talent like hers shouldn't be wasted. Her face lights up, making me smile. I give her hand a shake and push off from the ground, my wings still aching a little bit from the trauma they have been through.

As I glide through the air, my thoughts return to the attack by the Fallen. I've never seen so many attack at once. It's almost like I was lured into a trap, but it's hard to believe that they would plan something like that on their own. One thing about the Fallen, they are extremely selfish, taking pride in individual pursuits rather than team pursuits. I'm therefore suspicious that someone else is behind it. I have many an enemy, but not really any that I could see planning such a successful venture. I think I might stick to the buddy system for a while. Even with Torin's lackluster fighting skills, two people going against that many Fallen would have been much better than one.

I finally arrive at our compound, and by compound, I mean the giant palace the council calls our home. It's a towering, white, marble structure filled with arches and turrets that allow for easy flying in and out. It's located on a remote mountain peak. The locals in the area perpetuate stories that the mountain is haunted keeping most humans away from it. The palace has every luxury that can be made from the resources available on the planet, but it still lacks many of the things we enjoyed in Paradise. I fly in through one of the arches on the fifth level where a large gathering room is located. The whole council is gathered, many are shouting in a rare show of emotion. Angels aren't known for displaying much emotion. Surprisingly, Torin seems to be heading up the meeting. He's the last person that I would see filling a leadership void, and a little sliver of doubt starts to grow inside of me.

Lathan is the first to notice my presence. "Damon!" he cries, rushing over to me and placing a hand on my shoulder. "Where have you been?" he asks.

My attention is focused on Torin however. Lathan's shout alerted him to my arrival and I watch an array of emotions pass over his face. None of them the relief you would expect your best friend to display when you come back from the dead. He quickly schools his face however when he sees me watching and hurries over to me to stand by Lathan and clasp my shoulder as well. He then pulls me into what seems like a relieved hug.

"We were just about to send out a search party," Torin tells me. "We've all been so worried!"

I push aside my suspicion. There's no way that Torin had anything to do with this. I've known him since the beginning of my existence. I've never seen him do anything remotely in the league of what the Fallen attacks would entail.

I push my way into the middle of the room where my head of the council chair sits, a chair that Torin was occupying when I first arrived. "I was attacked by the Fallen," I tell the group bluntly once everyone is seated.

"We're attacked by the Fallen every day. What was so different that you would have trouble?" asks Lathan.

"I was attacked by at least a few hundred Fallen...at once," I answer. The room is silent for a moment before everyone begins talking simultaneously.

"How did you survive that?" calls out Arthur. "Even with your talent and abilities, odds like that would have been impossible."

I struggle with how to answer. Something inside of me wants to keep little Camilla a secret. Although I doubt anyone would voice disapproval of my fraternization with a human considering the circumstances, I know that everyone's opinion of humans mirrors my own, or at least my old opinion. It feels like it would be a slap in the face to the selfless gift that Camilla gave me to talk about her in this crowd.

"I'm not sure how," I answer, giving him at least a half truth since I don't know how I escaped that many Fallen. "I fainted due to the blood loss. It took a few days of going in and out of consciousness before I healed enough to return."

"A miracle," says Lathan, in awe. I nod reluctantly. Perhaps it was a miracle, but it was one that can be attributed to an awkwardly charming human girl rather than the heavens above.

Changing the subject, I begin giving out orders. "We will need to begin ongoing extra surveillance immediately. We will work in shifts with a team always patrolling. There is obviously something else going on besides a fight for souls if they are working together. Everyone is also to abide by the partner rule and make sure that someone is with them at all times when they go on missions."

"Why were you alone?" asks Lathan, looking at Torin angrily.

Before I can answer Torin pipes up. "We had heard of two situations that needed monitoring with the Fallen and decided to split up," he states hurriedly. "I never in a million years thought Damon of all people would be in danger. He's the best fighter of us all."

I look at him in disbelief. The fact that Torin is lying right now means that he wasn't asked to go help another team. I'm angry, furious in fact, because I know whatever the real reason was that he ducked out of rounds, it's not going to be a good enough excuse for the fact that I almost died. There's no getting around the fact that my best friend is lazy and selfish.

"I'm going to go to bed so that I can finish healing. Lathan, you and Heinrick are on patrol first. Wake me if you find anything suspicious before engaging. I was lured into a secluded glen in the middle of Blackwood Forest. Keep your wits about you at all times."

Everyone in the room nods in acknowledgment. A few come over to murmur good tidings to me before they leave the room. I intentionally avoid eye contact with Torin knowing that he will get the message that he is in trouble. I've always been so tolerant of Torin's faults, willing to overlook them because I've always believed he would do anything for me. My eyes are finally opening to the fact that I can't go easy on him anymore. If it had been anyone else ambushed on the council, they would have died.

I stalk out of the main room, my wings snapping out as I soar to the top level of the palace where my rooms are. There is no other word that fits my chamber better than opulent. Everything is of the nicest material available on earth and no expense has been spared to make sure I feel like the superior creature that I am. I feel a twinge of guilt when I think about Camilla's shithole shanty. I make a decision that I will see her again and I will make sure that her life improves.

A knock on the door rattles through the living room portion of my chambers. "Come in," I call out, knowing that it's Torin here to beg and worm his way back into my good graces.

Torin enters the room, his easy-going grin lighting up his face until he sees how serious my face is. "I just want to explain," he tells me.

"Explain why you lied and almost got me killed?"

"You can't stand there and act like I should have antici-pated that a few hundred Fallen were going to lure you into a trap and almost kill you. The most we've ever seen working in tandem was four or five, a number that's child's play for you."

I stare unflinchingly at him, unwilling to give him the forgiveness he wants at the moment. "Where were you really Torin?" I ask him again.

"There's a girl," he says shrugging his shoulders bashfully.

"You have got to be shitting me."

"She's not just any girl, she's the one," he argues. "She's my mate."

Despite my best intentions my heart softens a bit. I know realistically that whatever wood nymph or other creature he's hooking up with is most likely not his fated mate, Torin is a slut if there ever was one. Anything with boobs catches his eye. But he hasn't claimed that any of them are his fated mate before. So the fact that he is even thinking that is a big deal. As angels we only have one fated mate. We often spend millennia looking for them though so ultimately many angels have quite a bit of extracurricular experience before their one and only is found. I've never met anyone who even remotely made me question whether they are the one though.

"She's human," he spits out reluctantly.

I'm floored. It goes against every rule we've made for ourselves to have relations with a human, and there's no way that a human would be his fated mate. Or at least I think there's no way. It would just be another way that angels could be screwed over by the heavens if we were matched with a creature with such a small lifespan.

"What are you doing?" I ask him wearily. "If you're caught, you will be immediately kicked off the council."

"It's a risk I'm willing to take," he spits out defensively. I think of Camilla. There's a fragile elegance about humans that pulls at you. Perhaps Torin could fall in love with one.

"So you lied to me to go meet up with your lover?" I ask stubbornly, my rage abated somewhat.

"Brother," he says. "You know I would do anything for you, but I've been worried with the escalation of the Fallen attacks that somehow she would be caught up in the cross fire. I've been trying to find a safe house for her and a suitable hiding place became available that day. I never knew I was potentially choosing between you or her that day or I would have done it after we returned from patrols," he pleads with me.

That little seed of doubt from earlier grows just a bit larger. Not once has Torin ever seemed worried about the escalation of the Fallen attacks. He's far better of a liar than I've ever given him credit for. If he fooled me about all of that, what else could he potentially be hiding from me? My line of thinking is cut off by his next statement.

"You need to tell me everything that happened. I'm going to be haunted by this for the rest of my existence," he tells me dramatically, his face the picture of brotherly concern.

"They lured me in," I begin reluctantly. "I saw something flashing as I was flying my route and I went down to investigate. Rookie mistake."

Torin frowns sympathetically.

"As soon as I landed I realized something was wrong...it was too quiet. And that's when the attack began."

"But how did you survive?" he asks, sounding frustrated.

"I almost didn't," I admit reluctantly. "I was able to drag myself away when the Fallen tried to pile on top of me. I hid in a cave for probably a night, and then I tried to make my way home."

"Tried to make your way home? Didn't you succeed?" he asks.

"I missed the fact that I was right by a ravine and fell in a river. I almost drowned."

"You're leaving something out," Torin says, studying my face.

I'm torn. I tell Torin everything, I always have. And he's told me about his human lover so it shouldn't be a big deal to tell him about Camilla. I feel protective of her though.

"Damon?" Torin prods.

"I was rescued by a human girl," I reluctantly admit.

"You were rescued by a human?" Torin looks dumbfounded by my revelation and a little red in the face if I'm being honest with myself. "I can honestly say I would never have expected those words to come out of your mouth. Is she hot?"

I roll my eyes at him. Of course, that would be the first thing he asks. I feel a slice of guilt cut across me. Isn't that the first thing I usually ask?

"It's not like that. She's...different. She's an artist, and a healer. She rescued me even though my wings were out and I'm sure she was scared to death."

Torin is examining me closely. "You really care for this girl, don't you?" I say nothing. My feelings towards the little human are new and unfamiliar.

"Well that settles it. I want to meet her," he says suddenly.

"Not happening," I tell him. "At least right now. She's just found out that humans aren't alone in the world. I don't think now's the time to inundate her with more angels. Besides, I just put everyone down on lockdown until the Fallen situation has been managed. I doubt I will be able to get away to go visit her anytime soon."

"Well put me down on the visitor list whenever you decide to open it up for business," he tells me sarcastically, clapping me on the back. "Now go to bed, you look like shit," he throws over his shoulder as he strides out of the room.

Later that night I realize that he never told me the name of his human lover, or offered to let me meet her. What does that mean? I finally drift off to sleep, my dreams filled with the Fallen and a little red headed girl with a crooked smile.

Six

After

Eva's fallen asleep again. I find it amusing and endearing that she can't last through a movie without drifting off. I study her features, in awe as usual that any creature could look so perfect. Even in her sleep she has that soft glow that would signal to any supernatural with half a brain that she is one of us. The crazy thing about Eva is that she has a soul. I suppose in a horribly fucked up way it was probably good for her that she was with those terrible people for so long. There's no way that someone who looks like her wouldn't have had her head turned if she had constantly been worshipped for her entire life. Instead, because of, or in spite of her past (take your pick), her soul seems as perfect as her beauty.

All of my romanticizing doesn't make up for the fact that my dick is throbbing. It literally feels like I'm being tortured right now. It's the most pleasurable form of torture to kiss Eva, but I'm really hoping we can go further soon. I could tell she wanted more tonight but I'm so scared of pushing her further than she's ready for that I stopped us before anything could really begin. I've been trying to let her know every day how I feel so that she can be secure that I want her for more than her body. A part of me is also nervous to go further because I don't know what her asshole foster dad was like, and I have a sneaking suspicion he liked her in a way that went way beyond the usual familial bond. If I find out he did something ...I think I will hunt him down and kill him. I take deep breaths, trying to tamper the murderous rage that sometimes overtakes me ever since what happened to Camilla. It takes a moment, but the quiet sound of Eva's breathing lulls me into a deep sleep.

I'm following Eva down a brightly lit hallway. She turns her head to glance back at me, a loving smile on her face. She leads me into a room whose walls sparkle like they are embedded with diamonds. An enormous, sleekly, modern bed is situated in the middle of the room. I've been trying to avoid bedrooms with Eva as of late since it only makes it harder to delay taking the next step, but now she's led me right into the mouth of the beast. I notice for the first time that she's wearing one of my dress shirts. It fits extra-large on her but still manages to make my groin tighten with need at the sight of her sexy legs that go on for miles...and the thought that she could be naked underneath. She notices my predicament and a sly grin slides onto her face, her tongue peeking out to slightly moisten her bottom lip. I'm dying at this point. She walks slowly over to me, undoing one button at a time as she does so. I'm trembling in anticipation at this point, I've waited so long for anything to happen between us. Her sexy-as-sin skin is unveiled inch by inch as she slowly goes down the row of buttons. I've never seen someone make undressing so desirable. She finally gets to the point where the shirt is sliding down her shoulders, her delicate collar bone and the tops of her perfect breasts are now visible, and I salivate as she undoes the last crucial button...

"Damon?" calls a voice.

I wake up in a sweat. I'm so hard that I forget where I am for a moment. I blink, trying to get my bearings. Eva's looking at me with concern. The sexy white dress shirt from my dream is unfortunately nowhere in sight, although the tank top and cheerleading shorts she has on are nothing to cry about.

"Are you okay?" she asks. "You were shaking and talking in your sleep."

I'm beyond embarrassed that I just had the beginning of a wet dream while I was seated next to her and definitely don't plan on telling the girl of my dreams that I'm haunted at the thought of her naked body every time I close my eyes. "Fine, just a weird dream," I tell her. Sliding a pillow in front of the lower half of my body, I stand up, trying to not look awkward as I do so. I hold out a hand. "Ready to go to bed sleeping beauty?" I'm so glad that I don't avoid bedrooms like my dream self apparently does because sleeping with Eva is the highlight of my life. No matter how many times I have to take care of myself later on, nothing compares to the feel of her soft body nestled next to mine.

We walk into my massive bedroom. I like that it's become a habit that she always sleeps on the right side of my bed, that we've done this enough that there's a his and her side. I send up an internal prayer that I get the chance to do this forever. It's getting harder and harder not to be able to spend every night with her. I've promised her I'm not going to stop fighting for her, but it's still my deepest fear that Mason or Beckham will ultimately take her heart. She's facing me as I get into bed after her, flashing me that gorgeous smile that never fails to send butterflies coursing through me like I'm a teenager with my first crush rather than an ancient immortal being. I like that she reverts me to that. I've been so numb for so long that I didn't think I could ever feel any emotions again, let alone this crazy, all-consuming passion that I feel for Eva. She snuggles up against my chest, her head nestled right under my neck, and I just know that this is the pinnacle of a good life. I want this forever.

"What part of my godlike form are you painting today?" I ask Camilla as she purses her lips in concentration, ignoring my comments. She's been trying to paint me, but I'm having trouble sitting still today and I doubt today's session is going to go well. I never can stay away from the compound for very long before it would be noticed, so it's been taking her forever to finish my picture since she's only getting me to model for a little bit of time every visit. She's told me that she's only about halfway done. I pretend it's a nuisance, but secretly I'm excited to see what her talent does with my awe-inspiring looks.

Despite my restrictions to the rest of the council, I have snuck out a few times to bring Camilla food and supplies, and make sure she is doing alright. I bring her little tidbits from the supernatural world on these trips as well: a blanket that a warlock enchanted that always keeps the user at the perfect temperature; a water basin that I picked up in Turkey that never gets empty; and her favorite thing of all, paint I procured from a flower nymph. Camilla burst into tears when she saw the mesmerizing beauty of the paint. Flower nymphs have perfected the process of capturing the colors only seen in the wild. I had never been a painter, but I had gone through a period of time when I collected random things because of boredom and since flower nymph paint was a rare and highly prized commodity, I had gone out of my way to get some. Seeing Camilla's face when she used the first color on some of the canvases I had brought her was priceless.

She asks me question after question about the supernatural world. She's fascinated by the fact that all this time she thought humans were alone in the world when in fact angels, vampires, and demons are all around her all walking around unnoticed. It's amusing to see her different reactions to different creatures, or when I tell her why certain things are how they are.

"You're trying to tell me that earthquakes are caused by giants?" she looks at me incredulously.

I nod seriously. "They're temperamental buggers," I tell her. "Every so often the different tribes decide they hate each other and wage war. You can imagine what hundreds of 30 foot creatures crashing and stomping around would do to the land. The mountain giants cause avalanches as well." Her eyes widen and she looks impressed.

We have conversations about humans as well. After discovering they aren't all completely useless I pepper her with questions about why humans do certain things. "Explain to me why humans get married?" I ask her one day. "Life is so temporary, and humans don't have fated mates. Most human marriages I've seen are extremely unhappy. There a huge reason why the Fallen are so successful with taking human souls. It's easy to persuade a miserable person to do something terrible if you promise them it will make them happy."

She ponders my question for a moment and turns and gazes at me with a longing that I try to ignore. "I think that the promise of love, that there's one perfect person out there for us is the ultimate goal for everyone fated mate or not. Art started from the human's attempt to put love into a form. It makes sense that we would continue to try and find our match in another person. To love and be loved in return is the perfect ending for an imperfect soul."

She's still gazing at me, a little love-sick gleam in her eyes. "You said that humans don't have fated mates, does that mean that angels do?" she asks hesitantly.

"Yes we do," I tell her.

"Can she be a human?"

I hesitate, thinking of Torin's claim. I'm almost positive a human and an angel could never be fated mates, but even if it were possible, it's better to make sure she knows it's not her. "No, it's not possible," I tell her. She looks devastated for a second before she smooths out her face.

"But you haven't met your fated mate yet, right?" she asks.

I examine her face. Her jealousy and hate of my imaginary mate flashes like a spark across her face. Jealousy about other lovers is rarely found in angels. It's a hallmark of an angel once he has met his mate, but it rarely occurs outside of that situation. Jealousy in general amuses me. I can't even fathom what it would feel like to actually be jealous of someone. Not that I have to contend with situations that would breed it often. Most of the time I'm trying to pry my lovers off, not keep them to myself.

I sigh at the emotions that Camilla is broadcasting loud and clear. With every visit, my dilemma grows. I can sense that she's becoming more and more attached to me, but our visits are such a bright spot in my life that it makes me lonely just thinking about giving it up. Her eyes devour me no matter what I am doing, and she lights up whenever I arrive. I should stop visiting before it gets worse, but selfishness has always been a vice for me. It's my hope that if I continue to make sure she knows we are just friends that eventually some other human will catch her eye. I know that this a long shot though, no human would compare to an archangel in all of his glory. I need to just stay away...

"Alright, it's about time for me to head out," I tell her, shaking out my wings which are stiff from being still for so long. I'm tired of feeling like I'm disappointing my friend because I have no desire to take her to bed.

"You really have to leave already?" she asks, her eyes glossing over with a moisture that makes me uncomfortable.

"Yes," I reply firmly. "I'm not even supposed to be here, per my own rules."

"Why do you even come then?" she asks, her seldom used fiery attitude emerging.

"I want to make sure you're alright! You live alone in this pit of despair and I can almost see through you. You clearly don't know how to take care of yourself, much like the rest of your species."

Evidently that was the wrong thing to say. "Get out!" she cries, as she begins to throw various items at me. A cup narrowly misses my perfect nose when she throws that and a fork at me at the same time.

"I'll just see myself out," I bark at her, always having to get the last word in. I burst out the door and take flight, an icy wind nipping at my feathers and reminding me that winter is coming. Hopefully she will be reasonable at least in time for winter, so I can make sure she's set up comfortably. I fly away irritably, thinking about how this is just another example of how unreasonable humans are.

EIGHT

I'm going to stalk her I decide. I'm pretty sure that she's decided that she will just ignore me, and I'm not willing to let her do that. Wearing workout clothes should give me the perfect excuse to hover around her dorm room. I could just pretend that I was passing by on my run if she asks any questions. I get there early, around 5:00am, not knowing if she's an early riser or not. The campus is empty, the sun just blinking through the sky. An hour passes, and I feel somewhat stupid for getting here so early, there hasn't been anyone around. Most people don't get up at 5:00am who aren't being forced to. Eva's probably one of those girls who likes to get her beauty rest. I hear the door open for the first time this morning, and I immediately pretend to be stretching, keeping my head down so that if it's not Eva, I won't have a crazy fan on my hands.

I glance up tentatively, sure I wouldn't get so lucky, and almost fall over when I see that it's Eva. It's first thing in the morning and I know she doesn't have a stitch of makeup on, yet she looks ten times better than any supermodel I've ever seen who's all dolled up. I lose my breath for a second seeing that she's dressed up in a tiny pair of running shorts and a tank top. Her legs look like they go on forever and when she bends over, the slip of cleavage she flashes makes me salivate. She hasn't noticed me, and she continues stretching as I watch her in interest. After a few minutes, I start to feel like a creeper that I haven't announced myself yet.

"Good morning Eva," I call out to her. She turns around in surprise and stares at me suspiciously.

"What are you doing here?" she asks.

"I was just on my morning run when I saw you," I tell her, trying to give her my most winning grin. She seems to be relatively unaffected with most of the charm that makes others crazy, but it's all I have so I'll keep using it. "Want to join me?" I ask her, fingers crossed that she will give me even a second of her time. My smile widens when I see how obvious it is that she doesn't want to run with me. She's waging a war with herself and I'm fascinated to watch the play of emotions on her face. Finally, my wishes are granted.

"I'll run with you, but you're going to be disappointed," she tells me, the reluctance heavy through her voice. "I haven't been on a run in a long time." I glance over her stunning features, she has to be doing something because her body is perfect.

"I don't need to go super hard anyway because I have practice this afternoon," I tell her. I obviously don't mention that almost no amount of exercise could ever be enough for my immortal body to tire. She walks over to me and we start our run. I start off with a slower pace, but she still stays slightly behind me as we run, much to my chagrin. I was looking forward to being able to stare at her ass again. I try to act as a tour guide as we pass various sites, pointing out cool buildings, or telling her random facts about New York City. Eventually she begins to run next to me, matching my pace even as I speed up. We chat about random things but we're both mostly content to enjoy the sounds and sights of the city.

I glance over at her and notice that she hasn't even broken a sweat. She's either in really good shape, or my guess that she has some supernatural in her is correct. I speed up to test my theory. To my surprise and delight, she speeds up as well. We're both sprinting, and we keep up this pace mile after mile until finally I lead us to Central Park where we slow to a walk. I can't help but gape at her after I look at my mileage tracker. Nine miles practically sprinting, and she looks like it was nothing more than a walk in the park, metaphorically speaking.

"Do you realize how far we just ran?" I ask her. She shakes her head no, but there's a slight flash of panic in her eyes. "We ran nine miles. And you aren't even breathing hard." Her mind seems to be racing. She looks over at me, I'm sure noticing that I'm not sweating and don't seem to be struggling either. Something unsaid passes between us, like we both know that there's more to the situation, but we are agreeing not to talk about it. I'm honestly fine with that. Bringing in the fact that you're sort of a fallen angel comes with its own set of complications.

She smiles at me and I'm momentarily blinded. "I've always dreamed of going to Central Park," she tells me as she admires the trees that are just starting to turn a myriad of autumn colors. This has always been my favorite season and seeing her showcased with the lovely colors just makes me like it more. There's a coffee stand nearby, and I walk over to buy us some. As an angel I don't need the caffeine, but over the years I've become addicted to the taste and find myself having at least a few cups throughout the day.

"How do you take your coffee?" I ask her as she looks over the menu in the front of the cart. The guy manning the stand is staring at Eva with his mouth slightly open. He looks like he is about to start drooling. She seems to be oblivious, or maybe she's just used to the looks and can ignore it. I'm pretty sure that I'm going to continue to stare at her like that every time I see her, there's just no getting used to her beauty and the inner light that she radiates.

"As sweet as I can get it," she laughingly replies. "Just surprise me because the only actual coffee I've tried was a mocha latte."

That catches me off guard. "You've only tried coffee once?" I ask. She blushes and nods, a slight rosy tint hovering over her cheeks. I suddenly have the urge to take her to Leslie's. It's my secret spot where I escape from the throngs of people that want my attention all the time and where I can just be normal...or as normal as a supernatural being living among humans can be. "Alright, well this coffee stand will not do then," I tell her, throwing the disappointed coffee cart guy a twenty and grabbing her hand, racing to get a cab.

"Where are we going?" she asks, cutely giggling.

She has a naivety and wonder about her that makes me want to show her the world while simultaneously shielding her from it as well. "Introducing you to good coffee," I tell her with a wink, keeping her hand grasped in mine.

A little while later, and we arrive at Leslie's. She's quiet as we walk in, taking it all in. I'm surprisingly nervous to hear what she thinks. I've never taken a girl here and the namesake of the place, Leslie, is a little like a grandma to me. I want them to like each other.

"I've been coming to this place since I arrived in New York," I tell her. "It doesn't look like much, but there isn't a better coffee in the whole city." We're at the counter and I see Leslie's eyes widen when she sees Eva.

"Damon! Who is this angel you've brought with you today?" she asks.

I find the fact that she has referred to Eva as an angel hilarious seeing as how she's been serving an actual angel coffee for years, not that she's known that.

"This is Eva," I tell Leslie proudly. "She is a coffee novice, so I thought I would take her to get the best coffee in town. Eva, this is Leslie. She's run this coffee shop for thirty years. I've asked her to marry me several times, but she always tells me she's too old for me." It's a corny joke between us but Leslie has always been sweet on me despite her advanced age for a human.

We banter back and forth for a moment before Leslie asks Eva what she wants. Eva says she likes sweet things again, and I involuntarily think about how sweet she probably tastes...everywhere.

Leslie thankfully distracts me from where my thoughts and my pants were wandering as she begins to put together one of her famous concoctions. Eva and I both watch as she fiddles with various antique silver machines, Leslie believes in doing everything old school and always tells me that the old ways are the best ways. I agree with her since I'm older than most things. She finally finishes with a flourish and hands Eva a cup of coffee that's a lot more golden in color than anything I ever get. Leslie and I both watch as Eva tentatively tries a sip, closing her eyes for a second and moaning in delight as she absorbs the flavors.

"It's wonderful," she tells Leslie meaningfully after Leslie explains what it is. Leslie looks delighted. As she hands me my black coffee and a few honeybuns to take with us she whispers, "Don't let that girl go." I flash her a grin, so happy that my girls got along, and attempt to pay her in our usual back and forth. Leslie hasn't let me pay since someone "mysteriously" paid off the loan on the place, leaving her with the title free and clear. She somehow knows it was me and has refused my money ever since. Per usual, I still manage to leave a large tip that more than covers the cost of our food as we leave.

"It was nice meeting you Eva," Leslie calls after us.

We both smile at her in return, enjoying the delicious gifts she gave us. I can't help but reach for her hand as we walk, and I give an inward fist pump when she doesn't pull away. I decide to test my luck again by asking if she will let me run with her again the next day. She's quiet for a moment as if she's going over how our date went (I'm calling it a date at least).

"I would like that," she finally responds softly. I can't help but show my excitement and I'm practically giddy as we walk back to campus. I'm wondering if I can push for more time with her today when I notice that asshole Eric is waiting for us, looking furious. I listen to his frustration with amusement. The dude is digging himself a hole by acting so crazy. Eva makes me crazy too but I'm at least keeping it hidden from her. I decide to stir the pot even more and make it clear that I'm after Eva.

"Thank you for this morning," says Eva, very conscious of Eric's eyes on us.

"Can't wait until tomorrow," I tell her, not able to keep myself from brushing my lips across her smooth hand that I'm holding. She trembles slightly, hopefully from the palpable energy passing between us. At least that's how it's making me feel. There's something huge between us and in this case I'm not talking about my dick. I give her a wink, and then flash a salute at Eric. "See you at practice," I tell him as I saunter away, the glow of the morning settling on me like a cloak. For the first time in my long life, I wish that time would hurry up.

Nine

I take a deep breath and sigh. I feel listless, bored, my skin is crawling with the need to jump into action, to do anything. There's been a few more organized attacks in the few weeks that have passed since my return. None on the scale of the one launched against myself, but still enough that teams have sustained injuries. Per my own rules, the council teams have been alternating patrols. I've been keeping any teams not on patrol on lockdown to try and prevent injuries. I've been training everyone harder than ever before and I know that everyone is feeling the strain.

Torin looks over at me inquiringly when he hears my sigh. I shrug and skip a rock across the clear water of the lake in front of the palace where we just finished practicing drills. I watch as it disappears from view.

Against my better judgment, I've said nothing about Torin's extra-curricular trips to see his claimed love. A part of me is reluctant to try and interfere. If she really is his fated mate as he claims, then I would be damning Torin if anything I did caused her demise. As much as I am disappointed and a bit distrustful of Torin as of late, to lose your fated mate is a fate worse than death that I wouldn't wish on my greatest enemy. Still, he continues to disappear at odd intervals that make me wonder just where this secret hideout is that he procured for her. I'm also still weirded out about the fact that he hasn't discussed me meeting her yet.

He hasn't asked about visiting Camilla again though. I would probably bring him with me if he asked just to get her in a better mood. Torin usually can get anyone in a better mood with his antics. I haven't gone back. I'm not sure how long humans take to recover from being mad, and I haven't been in the mood to check and see. I miss her though. My friendship with Torin has changed since the attack, that kernel of doubt continuing to spread through me like a slow-moving poison as I have more and more begun to see him without the rose-colored glasses I viewed him with in the past.

When I witness him start to casually lie to other members of the Council about inconsequential things like if he ate the last piece of cake, or if he borrowed a weapon, I decide that I will just follow him on one of his trips just to stop myself from going crazy with suspicion. If he does in fact go to his human lover's house then I can continue to make excuses for him, maybe the stress of having to hide her and the fear of what the Fallen would do to her is driving him to be irrational. If he doesn't...well I'm not sure what I will do. Even with his shady actions, I still can't imagine what he could be doing on these trips that would be so bad that he felt like he couldn't tell me about them. We've seen each other at our best and at our worst, and I'm hard pressed to think of anything he could do that I couldn't forgive him for.

At dusk he sets out, looking around him carefully before he sails into the fading sky. I follow him at a distance. Torin never did pay close enough attention to his surroundings. It makes me think of the million and one times that I've had to swoop in and save his ass before he was killed by one of the

Fallen. He continues to glide through the sky at a swift pace, displaying a sense of purpose that I have seldom seen in him. Although Torin has never seemed to resent our mission like I do, his heart has never been in it and he often would try to do his best to sideline us from whatever our mission was for the day. I feel a shiver slide down my spine. Surely thousands of years was enough to really know someone, wasn't it?

After another ten minutes of flying his rapid pace begins to slow down, and he begins a slow descent down where there's a fair amount of tree cover. I slow down as well and land silently behind a tree some ways away from him. At first Torin is just pacing, and I become hopeful that he has just come here to think about something that is bothering him. A set of unfamiliar angels walk into the secluded grove Torin has landed in. They're both dressed in matching brown military wear, and I know that they are Fallen. They're loaded down with various weapons, and I immediately move to come to his aid, thinking that he will be overwhelmed. I pull out a small knife that I prefer for close combat, and prepare to step in. My steps are halted however when I see both Fallen give a small bow and beat their hand against their chest, an action that bespokes respect and allegiance. I would know, that's how most creatures usually approach me unless they are told otherwise. Torin has always made fun of me when it happens. He's never been one for pomp and circumstance. He seems to be soaking it up right now though.

I creep silently closer so that I can hear their conversation, dread squeezing my heart so thoroughly that I'm afraid I will start to choke.

"Master Torin, we attacked him as you requested. However..." The Fallen takes a deep breath as if steadying himself to deliver unwanted news. "However, there have been sightings of him. We believe he has survived."

"Of course he survived, you idiots!" states Torin angrily in a cold, authoritative voice that sounds nothing like my fun-loving best friend. "My question is, how did you let this happen? I made sure he was alone and that he would be caught off guard."

That seed of doubt that has been slowly developing ever since the attack bursts into bloom, suffocating in its enormity as my mind, and my heart, try to comprehend this bitter, blood curdling betrayal. I know who the "he" is they are talking about. My best friend, my comrade in arms, the one that has been a brother to me from my earliest memory, tried to have me killed.

"We've been escalating the attacks as you've requested, but we've been suffering high casualties as a result. We weren't able to send more than a few hundred of the soldiers you requested. I didn't think there was any way that even Commander Pierce would be able to survive such an onslaught of our best fighters. We were told that all of his injuries were so severe in scope that he couldn't possibly have survived," the Fallen explained hurriedly. "The few soldiers that returned from the attack all assured us that the blood he left behind was unfathomable. We aren't sure what happened after that, but I assure you our best efforts were given."

"I'll tell you what happened," Torin says in a silkily calm voice that at the same time is somehow laced with so much violence that it manages to send a shiver down even my back. "A human miscreant was able to save him somehow and nurse him back to health," he explodes. "We've gone backwards if anything since now he is intent on finding out who did this to him!"

Unexpectedly, Torin pulled his sword out of his belt, and slices through the Fallen's neck who had been speaking. To his credit, the other Fallen doesn't cower, but stands very still as if Torin is a predator in the wild and he could escape notice if he doesn't move.

Acting as if nothing had happened, Torin speaks to the surviving angel. "You're in charge now, I'll set a similar situation up again, but there can't be any mistakes this time. You know we need him out of the picture for our plan to succeed, and he's going to stop being so oblivious to what I'm doing if he manages to escape another large-scale attack on a mission I've abandoned him on. It took all the groveling I could stir up to alleviate his suspicions from the first attack," he says in a disgusted voice.

More words are spoken but I can't hear them. There's a faint buzzing in my ears and my heart seems to be beating so loudly that I can't focus on what's happening around me. Logically I know that I should keep listening in to hear more details about whatever "plan" Torin has going with the Fallen. However, the sting of Torin's betrayal has sliced into me and even in my perfected, often emotionless form, I can't recover.

Trying to still be mindful to keep my cover now that I know it's not just the Fallen I have to keep my eye on, I stalk through the trees, moving far enough away that I can take flight without being seen.

I fly aimlessly, my mind replaying the scene and Torin's callous words over and over again. I don't know what to do. My mind is jumbled trying to think of some other explanation for what I saw with my own eyes. Why would Torin join the Fallen? We have fought against them since almost our creation. I can't think of a single reason for his treachery. Torin may not have been passionate about our mission, but he's at least seemed to be in agreement that the Fallen aren't the good guys and should be destroyed if the opportunity presents itself. My thoughts swirl furiously in my head.

I find myself outside of Camilla's shack. She's hanging clothes on a line, humming to herself. She turns, startled at first until she sees its me. She then gives me a huge smile, all signs of her previous anger disappeared. Her smile turns to one of concern when she sees my state.

"What's wrong?" she asks worriedly as she jogs over to where I've landed.

"Everything," I say devastatingly, grateful to have someone to talk to. This thought sends me down another rabbit hole of mourning when I think of how I used to talk to Torin about everything. She begins to softly rub my back as she brings me inside.

She begins to search through some baskets for something. "Do you want to talk about it?" she asks, her voice muffled from her search.

I'm silent. I don't think I want to talk about it, at least not right now. I actually want to forget about the day's events. I want to go back to a time when Torin was just my fun-loving friend and my only worry was when my mission was going to be over, so that I could get back to Paradise. Now I face having to tell the council about what Torin is doing.

Camilla turns around holding a bottle of some elvish wine I had brought her on one of my visits. "Why don't we try this out?" she asks, a lilt in her voice that is a bit unrecognizable.

Thinking that drinking sounds like the perfect way to forget for a bit, I nod eagerly and quickly throw back the wine she has poured in the crude cup she offered me. Elvish wine is known for being the strongest drink around, even affecting supernaturals who have an extremely high tolerance to most forms of alcohol. I had brought it to her since she was so eager to learn about my world and she claimed she liked "a good stiff drink."

The evening flies by. Camilla has offered me cup after cup. I lose count of what number I'm on. Everything seems brighter and I feel like a weight has been lifted. I spin Camilla around the room. Her hair blows in the breeze, leaving a stream of red behind her. Camilla looks beautiful in the faded light, the shadows softening her angular face into something almost majestic. She gazes up at me like I am everything to her, and her adoration is a salve on my wounded soul. We're dancing now to a beat only we can hear. I collapse on the floor laughing, no longer able to stand up straight. She falls on top of me, her long hair cocooning us in a veil of flames. We stare at each other, and she lowers her lips to mine. I softly test out the feeling, the intimacy of the moment helping me to forget. Her clothes come off, and then mine, and then we're exploring each other's bodies as our breathing escalates. I forget everything but her soft moans as I touch her. They fill the air, combining with mine in a cacophony of sounds that is both lovely and terrible.

TEN

I wake with a start. Camilla lays sleeping, her head nestled against my chest. I gently move out from under her, watching as she briefly stirs and then returns to a deep sleep. I walk over to the hole cut into the side of the house to provide light and stare out. What did I do?

I feel anxious, flustered...guilty. We are strictly forbidden from interacting with humans at all, and here I've just fucked one, and not just a random one, but the only human friend I've ever made. Worst of all, I know that what just happened meant far more to Camilla than it did to me. Her whispered "I love you," as she came idles in my mind. It never should have happened. Camilla has become a prized friend, but I'm not even attracted to her. Now I have two terrible situations on my hands, both with my best friends. I hear the blankets rustling.

"Damon?" she asks me questioningly. I'm sweating, I have no idea what to say, what to do about this situation. Like a coward I walk back towards the makeshift bed. I try to smile at her reassuringly and pull her close to my body after flipping her around to face the other way so that she isn't looking at me. I listen as her breaths grow deeper, signaling that she has fallen back to sleep. The rest of the night I lay awake, my mind burdened with both the situation with Torin, and the trouble I have found myself in.

Dawn comes sooner than I would like. I've been going over what I'm going to say to Camilla. Maybe I can just blame it on the rules of being a Guardian. I mean we've never talked about what I actually am beyond that of an ordinary angel. She'll understand right if I explain that to sleep with a human is one of the foulest things that an angel can do? The guilt sits like a lead weight in my stomach. Although *I* know the seriousness of what has just happened, I'm sure explaining it *to her* will sound like a hollow excuse.

She's still in my arms when I feel her start to stir. She twists in my arms until she faces me, a content and happy look on her unusual face. I study her features, trying to see if there is anything inside of me that feels more than I would for a treasured friend. There's nothing there. Although I would readily admit to anyone that I'm very shallow when it comes to looks, there is more that I'm hoping for in my eventual mate. I have never been in love before. I have never found that certain, indescribable spark in someone else that makes me want to vow everlasting love and settle down. Despite the fact that I find Camilla interesting and unusual, I can't find it in me to feel something deeper.

I'm about to tell her that this was a terrible mistake when she gives me a soft kiss on my lips.

"Last night was the most amazing night of my life. I didn't know...I didn't know if you would come back, or that there was even the chance something like that could happen between us. It felt like everything I've ever dreamed about, being with someone you love and who loves you back. I've wanted this for so long. I can't believe it really happened."

A look of vulnerability crosses over her features.

"You wanted this right?" she asks softly.

In my mind a steady slew of curses is rattling through my brain at my life, Torin, alcohol...basically everything at the moment. Not knowing or wanting to answer I smile and kiss her quickly, hoping that it will be good enough for right now until I figure out what the hell I'm going to do. We stay on the hard, worn mattress that she sleeps on, her head nestled against me as she traces things on my chest. I idly play with her hair as I wait for a good time to leave. What's the most horrible thing about this situation is now I'm going to have lost two best friends.

Finally, when I feel like I have done the polite thing long enough, I gently lift her off of me so that I can get up. We are both still completely unclothed, and I avert my eyes from her form as I quickly get dressed. My clothes smell like strong alcohol and a wave of nausea passes over me. I hope that my healing abilities will give me a break and get rid of this hang-over sooner rather than later. At this point, the only plus of the morning has been that she hasn't tried to get me to sleep with her again. It's one thing to get an erection when your drunk and attraction can be imagined, it's a whole other beast to fake attraction in the bright light of the day.

"Well, I've got a long day ahead of me," I tell her awkwardly. She's braiding her long, bright, auburn hair and watching me with a studious expression. I'm worried she can read my mind about just how much I want to get out of here. I see something wild in her eyes and wonder what she's think-ing. She stands on her tip toes and lays a soft kiss on my lips. The uneasiness rises higher within me. I normally would have no problem telling someone I wasn't interested, that this was just about the sex. But Camilla saved my life. She's one of the only friends I have, especially now...especially now that Torin has betrayed me. I'm just going to have to tell her later I decide, swiping my thumb gently across her cheek in response to her kiss.

"Will you be back soon?" she asks quietly.

I frown at the question. We've never had a relationship where there has been scheduled visits. I've flown to visit her when I feel like it or when I have a chance. Is this a human thing? I try to think if any of the girls I've been with before have needed to see me at certain times. Nothing comes to mind and I'm not sure what the right move is. "I have patrol for the next few days. I don't usually take afternoons off to drink (or fuck)," I respond, obviously leaving the "fuck" part out. That same wild look rises to the surface on her face. Her panic is tangible in the air. She takes a breath and then a blank look covers her features.

"Well, I'll see you soon," she tells me, giving me a casual wave before she walks back inside her house.

I'm more confused than ever. What the ever-loving fuck just happened? Deciding to take the opportunity to leave nevertheless, I push off the ground and take flight. The gravity of what I've just done lays like a heavy mantle over my head. If anyone finds out... They just won't find out I decide. It's not going to happen again. With my mind made up, I speed through the air. One problem down, one to go.

Eleven

I'm weary as I touch down in front of Camilla's poor excuse for a house. It's been two long months of constant conflict with the Fallen. As soon as I left Camilla after that last disastrous visit, I was pulled into a council meeting. I'm sure that the others could smell the stench of sex and alcohol all over me, but luckily no one made a comment despite the strict rules I had placed on the group. We've all been there. Maybe not with a human, but the other members of the counsel aren't exactly virgins and I'm sure how rough I looked was preventing any pushback. We've all been stressed. I'm sure they have been finding ways behind my back to "blow off steam" as well.

The topic of conversation of the emergency meeting: Torin has disappeared. Everyone is wondering whether Torin has been captured by the Fallen. I can't take them discussing the need to "get back our brother" for very long before the truth is spitting out of my lips.

"Torin is leading the Fallen attacks," I announce, the council going silent at my proclamation.

"Damon, do you need more sleep? You sound irrational," Jarbin inquires, shock written across his features.

"I don't know why, and frankly after finding out that he was responsible for my attack I don't really care why, but he has indeed betrayed us," I answer, a twinge of melancholy weaving through my words.

"What is the proof of this?" calls out Marco. He and Torin had always bonded over their position as the weakest on the Council, although Marco's skills had always seemed heads above Torin's. Was Torin's lack of skill even real?

"I followed Torin yesterday. He's been engaging in a number of suspicious behaviors as of late, the first being that he told me that Jarbin had asked him to accompany you two on a patrol. This led to me patrolling by myself and the attack that I barely survived. When I came back, he told me that he had actually found his fated mate and had been moving her to a place that would be safer from the Fallen during the patrol and hadn't wanted to tell me because his mate was human."

"He claimed he had a fated mate who was human?" asks Heinrich, a note of distaste and skepticism laced through his voice.

"He did. I finally followed him after I had caught him lying to each of you about small things. He seemed to be doing it just to see if he could get away with it. It was enough to trigger my suspicion enough to find out if this mate existed."

The whole room is now hanging on my every word. I take a deep breath and try to keep my voice from shaking as I get to this next part.

"I trailed him to some woods not far from here. Two Fallen met him there. They talked about their attack on me, and Torin cut off one of the Fallen's head for failing to kill me. He then told the other one he would be setting up another opportunity for them to slaughter me. I should have stayed and listened to more of their plan...but I couldn't."

No one tells me how stupid I was or calls me a failure for failing to get more information or even apprehend Torin right then. They all know what Torin's disloyalty means to me. Everyone is in a state of shock as they weigh my words. Angels from Paradise become Fallen all the time, but not since Lucifer has an angel in such high standing willingly plunged from grace.

After a moment, Jarbin finally finds his words. "What are we going to do?" he asks.

"We're going to find him, and then he will be put in front of the tribunal for them to decide his fate," I state decisively. We spend the next few hours mapping out a plan for war and how we are going to find Torin. The next few months have been filled with skirmishes against the Fallen at every turn, but there's been no sign of Torin.

Coming back to the present, I call out "Camilla?" through the front door of her shack that's been left wide open.

"Damon!" she cries from inside, running out and almost knocking me down as she flings her arms around me.

"Umph," I say roughly. "It's good to see you too." All of a sudden her tiny fists start beating against my chest and she bursts into tears. I'm very confused.

"Where have you been?" she cries. "It's been three months. How could you do that to me?"

A feeling of dread passes over me. Obviously, humans form attachments much quicker than angels. I was hopeful that she had moved on. It's not like this is the first time that I haven't dropped by in a few months since that fateful day that she saved my life. I gently grab her shoulders and move her back so that I can look at her face. She looks...fuller somehow. Her face is slightly more rounded. I glance down the rest of her body in confusion. Everything looks more rounded. She even has boobs suddenly, which really would have made the night we fucked a lot more enjoyable now that I think about it. She was flat as a board if I remember correctly, the whole night is kind of a daze.

"You've gained weight," I say bluntly. I've been bringing her bags of food ever since we met since she was nothing but skin and bones. I guess it's finally started working.

"We need to talk," she says stiffly. She's stopped crying, but now there's a nervous tension around her eyes that's making me nervous. She takes my hand and I follow her inside. She turns and faces away from me, but I can still see the rigidness in her shoulders that tells me I'm not going to like whatever she has to say.

"We're having a baby," she says bluntly, finally turning to look at me. I'm flabbergasted for a moment, and a wave of nausea passes over me. Just as quick, I regain my senses and relax. "That's impossible," I tell her calmly. Her eyes widen. I'm sure that was the last thing she expected to come out of my mouth.

"What do you mean that's impossible?" she says severely, her tone wounded and rough.

"I mean that an angel can only have a child when they purposely choose to have a child, and that night that we..."

"That night we made love," she said interrupting me.

"The night we drunkenly hooked up," I corrected her harshly. "I did not choose to have a child."

"How do you know you didn't "purposely choose" if you claim you were so drunk?" she said, a rising note of panic threaded throughout her voice.

"It's not something that can be chosen while impaired," I attempt to patiently explain. "When an angel chooses to procreate it's a sacred and dangerous thing and can only be done with the right person. We're forbidden from procreating from humans because there's always the chance we could create a monster instead of a child. What would be born from a union of the two of us would be a new type of being. Angels are born of fire, so what they create through sex, is something totally different."

"I don't care what you are saying. This is your child," she states, a mad gleam in her eyes. Suddenly, her face is wiped of emotion, and she turns around and walks inside. Her frequent leap from emotion to emotion has my head spinning to keep up as usual. I follow her, hoping I can talk some sense into her. She picks up a pile of wool from inside one of her trunks. It's a faded pink color, and it appears to be taking the form of some sort of blanket that I'm sure will be used for the baby. Humans don't have the technology yet to be able to guess gender. I push out my senses a little bit though to see if I can see what the baby is. A sad, aching feeling wells up inside of me. It is a little girl, but it's definitely not mine. Who has she been with? I don't feel any jealousy, just worry, and a little anger that the real father isn't here taking care of his family right now.

I retract my senses and stare at her, a sick feeling building up inside of me. I search her eyes, hoping this is all a joke. If I wasn't such a screw up we would be celebrating right now. I would be ecstatic that my friend had found a lover and would soon be the mother of a child that she could share all of her wonderful talents and loving nature with. Instead, I've poisoned her, this precious, talented, fragile girl.

I try again. "Camilla, can we talk about this? Who else have you been with?"

She's humming to herself as she knits, ignoring my questions. I pull at my hair, exhausted from the last months of campaigns and ill prepared to take on a crazy pregnant human. "I'm leaving right now, but we're going to talk about this when I return. You need to be moved to a better place to live, along with a myriad of other things."

I wait for her to give me any response, but she continues to hum the same tune, a happy melody so annoying considering the situation that it feels like I'm being drilled in the head. I stalk out of her hovel and fly off, aggression and frustration beating off of me in waves.

TWELVE

BEFORE

I'm on patrol the next day when I finally see Torin for the first time. I'm exhausted, up all night thinking about what has happened to Camilla and how it can be fixed. I plan on going to see her today after my round of patrols. I plan on either attempting to talk to her or get her mental help from one of the human mind healers I've heard of, but I'm not going to leave until she's okay.

Heinrich is with me, and he's actually the one to first point at Torin hovering in the air far ahead of us, along with a few other angels, assumedly Fallen ones. Ignoring my inner voice that tells me it's a trap I race ahead, Heinrich calling after me, to confront Torin. Months of pent-up rage erupt at once as I run full force into him. The blow sending him hurtling to the ground while his Fallen comrades rush after him. I follow behind and am flying so fast that I land on the ground at the same time as Torin, who manages to get his wits about him in time to stop himself from crashing to the ground.

Torin looks a bit shaken but assumes a cocky posture, so different from the Torin I've always known. He flashes a grin at me, lazily pointing at something behind me. I whirl and see that Heinrick is being forcibly subdued by ten Fallen. His wings have a knife in each one, pinning him to the tree. He looks like he is in agony.

"We should think before we act, shouldn't we?" Torin asks delightedly. "I'm so glad that we've finally reunited. I've missed my best friend."

"Fuck you," I tell him unhelpfully.

"No, let's save the fucking for Camilla, shall we?" he asks me with a smirk.

My heart freezes. "What do you mean by that?" I ask him, afraid of the answer.

"Well, let's see. I know that you've fucked her...and I know that I've fucked her." He looks around the glen where we are all gathered. "Anyone else joined in on the fun? I know she's a human, but they've got to be good for something."

Everyone is silent. Even Heinrich has stopped thrashing and yelling, the shock of Torin's statement rendering him mute.

"How did you find her?" I ask in a stiff, calm voice.

"Well unfortunately you left your knife behind when you decided to spy on me and ruin all my fun plans for you," he says, pulling out the small knife that I had completely forgotten about in the haze of finding out about Torin's duplicity.

"I guess it really must have distracted you finding out that we weren't bffs after all," he laughingly mocks me, sticking out his lip in a mock pout. "I know you're usually a stickler for detail."

I move at him suddenly and am only stopped from driving my fist in his face when I hear Heinrich give a cry of a pain as one of Torin's henchman pushes a knife deeper into his wing.

"Ah, Ah, Ah, we mustn't lose our temper. Good things never happen when we let our emotions rule us. Like when you had sex with your disgusting little human friend. You somehow made it look so hot that I forgot all about burning her little hut down with the two of you inside of it. After you left she was so very depressed. Don't worry brother, I stepped in to raise her spirits. A simple potion to glamour my face and she thought you were returning for round two a few nights later," he says, shooting me a pleased grin.

There's a rock in my stomach now. Camilla wasn't crazy. She really thought that she was having a baby with me. She must be so confused and distraught right now. I stare at him. I've had months to get used to the fact that Torin isn't who I thought he was, but the angel standing in front of me is worse than I comprehended, he's more a demon than an angel. The depths of his duplicity are astounding. You would think thousands of years would be enough to know someone, and yes, I am being facetious.

"So, the baby is yours then I'm assuming? You know then what you've created."

"Yes, but she doesn't know what I've created. Imagine her surprise when a little monster pops out a few months early. She's going to be so very disappointed when she realizes her love child with her beautiful angel isn't a child."

I shake my head in disgust and fury, remembering how Camilla's face was filled with so much love as she stroked her stomach that day.

"We were meant to rule this planet, not to be subservient to the humans. You hate them too but look at you, wasting your life away following the rules we were given by a Paradise we can't return to. I'm going to do what you could never do," he tells. "Once I destroy you, my army will ensure that the proper beings are in charge and we are treated like the gods we are on this planet." Torin has a sick look of satisfaction on his face.

The villain always has to brag about his plan at some point, although in this case, it was pretty easy to figure out.

"If I were you I would run away right now, because as soon as Heinrich is let go I'm going to rip your heart out right after I rip off your wings one by one," I tell him. "The only way you're ever a ruler will be in your dreams."

There's a shiver of fear in his eyes that he struggles, and fails, to hide. There's only ten soldiers in the glen with us. Torin knows that today is a battle he's not going to win.

He gives me a cool smile. "See you soon," he calls as his wings push him up to the sky. "Give my regards to Camilla."

I turn immediately to help Heinrich, there's only five Fallen left, the cowards. It takes me only a few minutes to tear off their heads and free him. He grasps my shoulder in gratitude, but I can tell he is intentionally not meeting my eyes. No doubt finding out the illustrious leader of the council has dallied with a human has thrown him for a loop.

"Let's get back to the others," I gruffly tell him. Heinrich can barely stay afloat in the air because of the cuts in his wings. I half carry him back to the compound where the rest of the council are waiting.

"I'm not going to say anything," Heinrich tells me out of the blue right before we fly in. I look at him in question. "You saved my life today. I'll keep this secret."

"It's not how he made it sound," I tell him, annoyed.

"Did you fuck a human or not?" he asks.

"Well yes, but it was under extenuating circumstances, and I was very upset at the time."

"Dura lex, sed lex," he tells me seriously, a hint of pity in his eyes. I grit my teeth and nod. What can I say? Disobedience to the laws are what set the Fallen apart from the rest of the heavens. As we fly into the main common area, I'm struck with a sense of deja vu. It feels like every time I come in here the rest of the council are waiting for me wearing anxious, worried expressions.

"You've been gone far longer than a routine patrol," said Jarbin, stating the obvious.

"Yes, well as you can see we ran into our little brother," I tell him sarcastically, pointing to Heinrich, and heading into the hallway.

"Where are you going?" demands Jarbin as I leave the room.

"Planning a murder makes me hungry. Heinrich can update you," I tell him, as I leave without looking back. After grabbing something to eat from the kitchens I return to my quarters to lay on my bed and imagine all the ways that I can kill Torin. A prickle of unease passes over me and my thoughts are drawn to Camilla all of a sudden. I sit up. How could I have left her there knowing that Torin knows where she lives? I curse myself and fly out the window, rushing to get to Camilla's. As I fly the unease builds up inside of me until its practically choking me. Angels often have the gift of sensing when something is wrong, although my gift obviously picks and chooses what it tells me.

I land in front of her house. There's a bite in the air and I'm reminded again that I need to get Camilla somewhere better for winter...and figure out what to do about the demon she's carrying.

"Camilla?" I call out urgently, expecting her to come running out like she usually does when I visit her. But there's nothing this time. Every pore is filled with dread as I approach the entrance. I close my eyes before I walk in, intrinsically knowing that my whole life will never be the same again once I open them. After a minute I open my eyes and walk slowly in, sinking to my knees at the sight in front of me.

Camilla is laying on the ground, a look of horror splashed across her face. A solitary cut has been made across her throat, and the blood has stained the clay dirt all around her. Her auburn hair is matted in the blood, dying it a much darker red than usual. I reach out a hand, knowing that it's too late and there won't be a pulse. She had been painting, I notice idly. There's a paintbrush still gripped in her hand and a canvas is laying beside her upside down. My hands are trembling as I reach to pick up the canvas.

I've never cried before, but I cry that night. Sobbing and cursing at the heavens to a god I don't believe in anymore as I hold the painting of myself that Camilla was working on when she was slaughtered. In the right bottom corner Torin had signed his name, as if there was a doubt in my mind who was responsible for her death. She painted me as she wanted me to be, my eyes brimming with a love I've never felt, gazing at someone not visible in the picture. I mourn the fact that she never knew what it felt like for someone to love her like that.

I dig her grave slowly, shovel after shovel, the motion therapeutic in its repetition. The echo of the metal hitting the ground reverberates through the clearing. When it's finally done, I lay her gently in the hole, kissing her lips gently before I do so, and laying the magical blanket on top of her that I had gotten for her. I also lay the baby blanket next to her that she had been knitting. My heart is full of grief, but I hope that maybe in Paradise her child will be born whole, unblemished from the curse that angels bring to humans. I riddle the ground with my tears as I fill the hole. There's no one there to say goodbye, and I realize the truly sad part of this whole thing is that no one would be here even if they knew she had died. This wonderful talented creature had spent her life always alone.

I gather her paintings carefully and then I burn the house down until there's nothing left but ashes.

THIRTEEN

There's a cold fury in my heart once I reach the compound. The rest of my brothers are sleeping, and I wake them up calmly, simply telling them that it's time. I somehow know where Torin is as we take off, loaded down with weapons for war. Our favorite meadow by the river seems like the perfect place for the pompous Judas to plan my demise right under my nose. I haven't been back there since I found out about his betrayal.

The council follows me grimly as we sail through the sky. Soon my premonition proves right when we see a litany of tents peppering the landscape ahead. It looks like Torin has assembled an army of at least a few thousand Fallen. I marvel at first that he was able to do such a thing, but then I remember I don't really know him at all.

The sun is just making an appearance as we begin our attack. Torin may have been able to assemble an army, but his pompousness obviously prevented him from making sure there were enough guards awake while his army slumbered. The few guards he left are easily handled before they can make a sound. We begin making our way through the camp, slaughtering the Fallen we encounter as we search for Torin.

A scream pierces the dawn as one of the Fallen finally is able to sound the alarm before he is killed. Fallen rush from their tents, wiping the sleep from their eyes as they mount their attacks. I see Heinrich kick a burning log from a dying fire into a tent, immediately setting the tent on fire. I give a wicked grin as I watch the fire spread quickly into surrounding tents. The air is filled with smoke, ash, and blood.

I finally see Torin's tent. It's obviously his because it's the largest and most lavish of them all. I quickly dispose of the guards standing outside and watch a disheveled, confused looking Torin make his way out of the entrance of the tent. A barely dressed river nymph following behind him. He sees me one second too late as I attack him from the side, sending him tumbling to the ground.

I use one hand to hold him down on the ground, while the other one rips off his wing as he screams in agony, tears rolling down his face. I can faintly hear his little friend screaming in the background.

"Why?" is all I can ask him as I stare in my old friend's eyes.

"You were always better than me," he says simply, a look of crushing defeat in his eyes as he realizes this is the end. I recognize that there's nothing else to say. Jealousy has motivated every action that has led to this moment. This was never going to be a fair fight. Torin may have faked many things, but he couldn't fake how poor of a warrior he is. Hiding from me is the only way that he's lasted this long.

"Goodbye brother," I tell him solemnly before tearing Torin's heart from his chest, just as I promised him I would. The battle comes to a halt. Torin's wing lays beneath me. His feathers litter the ground everywhere I look. His blood has made small pools all around me and my hands and arms are stained red from where I pulled out his heart. I thought that killing him so savagely would make me feel better, would help to absolve the guilt I feel over Camilla's death, but I feel nothing. It's like I've become numb to any emotion. I stare around at my surroundings. The air is smokier than before as the fire Heinrich set ravages the tents. I can taste the iron tang of blood from the slaughtered Fallen. I expect there to be screams, but everything seems absolutely quiet. My hands are shaking, the adrenaline of the battle coursing through my veins.

The other Fallen scatter after seeing Torin's fate. The cowards didn't want to risk their own lives after seeing their leader so brutally murdered. I don't expect there will be much trouble for awhile beyond the usual eternal wrestle for human souls that's we've always had to deal with.

I guess I can't say we anymore.

Looking at my hands I know that there isn't a place for me with my brothers anymore. I don't even know if they would actually kick me off the council considering the circumstances, but I know I don't belong there. My brothers look exhausted, many of them covered in bruises and blood. Some are looking at me shocked after witnessing me tearing out Torin's heart. I look at Heinrich, standing nearby, and give him a nod. He understands that I'm leaving and he is to tell the rest of the council what I've done so they don't come after me. I kneel and close Torin's eyes, hoping against my will that angels don't cease to exist after they die and that he will find the peace after death that he couldn't in life. I then push off from the ground and ascend through the air.

I've fallen.

Time passes slowly. The centuries drip by, the memories never fading. At times I see my brothers in the distance, most likely on some mission. They pass by without a glance. I'm nothing but a cautionary tale to them, a story told at midnight about their fallen comrade who flew too close to the sun and got burned.

Mason and Beckham have become my new brothers. Their continued loyalty despite my tendencies to try and push them away at every turn has helped ease the bitterness that Torin left in me. Despite my best intentions, sometimes I still think of him and mourn the loss of our friendship, and who he ended up becoming. I try not to think about Camilla, and specifically make it a life rule never to fuck or fraternize with red heads.

If there's anything that I gained by becoming "fallen" so to speak, it's the freedom to do whatever I want. As long as I'm not going after souls, something which I have no desire to do, I'm left alone, free to pursue my own devices. I've chosen sports and sex. Sports have evolved in every century. I've dabbled in them all until finally humans came up with something that I fell in love with...football. Sex, well it is what it is. I gorge myself in it, perhaps a part of me hoping that the small amount of intimacy that comes with every encounter can fill the hole inside of me.

An excess of sex, fame, and football is all that fills my shallow life until the night I first dream of her.

"You're an angel," says Eva suddenly. We're laying on a mattress I pulled up to the rooftop garden. The lights of the city are so bright that it's almost impossible to see the stars. Eva wanted to try though, so here we are.

"I think we've already established that," I reply with a slow grin, turning my body so that I'm facing her instead of the sky. Her face has a dreamy look upon it as she stares at the firmament above us. Clouds float across the black expanse laid out like a tapestry. The moon is full tonight. I put a note on the mental list I keep, to take Eva out to the Hamptons so she can see what a real full moon looks like. I get the feeling that she hasn't seen very much in her life.

"Have you met God?" she asks me in a soft, vulnerable tone that makes me want to pull her close and reminds me of a conversation I had long, long ago.

"No, I haven't," I reply just as quietly. It's always been a sore spot for those in the upper hierarchy of angels. We know that paradise exists since we have been there, but we're never considered good enough to be in the deity's presence. That's something that is reserved for the humans we are forced to protect. My mind veers away from its bitter path when I see the look of shock on her face. I kiss her nose, and she scrunches it up in indignation. I see the way she melts though. I would do anything to keep that look on her face. I lean in to kiss her, but she rolls farther away on the mattress playfully.

"Uh, uh, uh," she tells me, wagging a finger in front of my face. "You and the others never want to have serious conversations about your past lives or where you've come from. Tell me something no-one else knows about you, something that can just be for us," she begs.

I stare at her for a moment, mulling over what to tell her. Most of my life before her seems to be black and white, a litany of excess, and selfish mistakes. I must take too long, because she flips over on her back again to stare at the night sky.

I try to picture Paradise in my mind. For so long I kept it there, a symbol of everything I had lost. It doesn't seem so shiny anymore I realize. There's no sharp pang in my chest, no longing for something I can't have. I feel...like I'm right where I'm supposed to be. I know this change is because of Eva. Paradise would be hell without her by my side. She reaches out her hand to grab mine and that sense that I'm home only increases. I mull over what to tell her. She already knows the really big fact that I'm an angel, and there's a million inconsequential things I could tell her, but a part of me wants her to hear the worst part of me. I want her to know the dark ugliness that sits inside of me so that I know if she really cares about me...if she really loves me. Words she hasn't said.

"Before I met Mason and Beckham, I had two best friends," I begin slowly. I can feel her interest and her gaze, but I can't bring myself to look at her as I continue. "They are both dead because of me. I killed them." I've never uttered those words out loud, not even to Beckham and Mason, and it's almost a relief to finally get the words out.

The silence is suffocating as my words hang between us.

"You killed them?" she finally asks, in a hesitant, quivering voice. "You, personally?"

"I only killed one of them, but the other one, a human girl, she died because of me and my selfishness." She's still, weighing her words or options probably. Talk about ruining a date, I'm evidently a pro.

"Tell me about them," she finally says. I weigh what to say and finally decide that it would be easier to show her. "Give me a moment," I tell her as I make a call. I'm grateful once again for the fact that my name can get me anything in this city. After I finish my call, I hold out my hand to her. She looks at me curiously but takes it and follows me down to the car. We're both dressed in lounging clothes, but since we will be the only ones in the museum, I don't think it matters.

Shelton takes us to a side entrance of the Metropolitan Museum of Art. I don't say anything in the car, my thoughts vibrating with echoes of the past. Eva, sensing my mood, says nothing as well, waiting patiently for me to talk when I'm ready.

We greet the guard who's waiting at the door and he motions us in, giving us a few rules and telling us we have two hours before we have to leave. I nod and walk quickly to our destination, pulling Eva behind me. I know exactly where to go.

We walk to one of the rooms dedicated to artwork from unknown authors, and I stop in front of a brilliant painting of a sunset. Eva gasps in amazement at it, her eyes widening at its beauty.

"This was painted by a little red head named Camilla," I begin...

Epilogue

A buzzer sounds, shaking me out of my reverie. I walk over to the door reluctantly and press on the speakerphone. "Who is it?" I ask rudely, not wanting any visitors, but not wanting to ignore it just in case it's Eva somehow.

"Open the damn door you stupid angel!" comes an annoyingly familiar voice.

"Go away!" I tell Lexi brusquely. I've never trusted Eva's red-headed devil of a friend. She's tried way too hard to ingratiate herself with Eva, and she's always lurking around everywhere I look.

"Damnit Damon, let me in!" she screams through the intercom. I mute the sound and stroll over to the couch. There's a large spreadsheet laying on the coffee table where all of my notes about where Eva could be have been written down. I'm pouring over them when the front door suddenly crashes open. The force of the door knocks some decorative glass vases off of the counter, and they crash to the ground, shattering into a million pieces. I jump up and stare in shock as Lexi strolls through the door. She looks wild and pale, and there's a faint blue glow coming out of her hands.

"Those were expensive," I tell her dryly.

She looks at all of the glass laying on the ground and shrugs. "I told you I had something to tell you," she says nonchalantly, acting like she hadn't just crashed through my front door uninvited.

"Please, do make yourself comfortable," I say sarcastically as she takes a seat on my couch, curiously reading over the notes on my spreadsheet. "Well? Are you going to tell me whatever was so important that you had to break into my home to deliver the information?"

She has a triumphant look on her face as she stops perusing the notes and glances up at me. "I know where Eva is."

Continued in Forbidden Queens ...

Definitions

Dura lex, sed lex: The law is harsh, but it is the law.

Author's Note

Thanks for taking the time to read Damon's story. When I was first creating the Fated Wings Series, Damon was the first of Eva's love interests that I came up with. I have always loved stories involving fallen angels. So much so that originally, all of Eva's men were going to be fallen angels! That changed...as you will see in Forgotten Queens when Eva's identity is finally revealed...maybe.

If you've enjoyed getting to know Damon, please leave a review on Amazon to give me further motivation to keep the story going. As I've said before, reviews are the lifeblood of authors, and I read all of them.

Visit my **Facebook** page to get updates.

Visit my **Amazon Author** page.

Visit my **Website**.

Sign up for my **newsletter** to stay updated on new releases, find out random facts about me, and get access to different points of view from Eva and the guys.

ABOUT C.R. JANE

A Texas girl living in Utah now, I'm a wife, mother, lawyer, and now author. My stories have been floating around in my head for years, and it has been a relief to finally get them down on paper. I'm a huge Dallas Cowboys fan and I primarily listen to Taylor Swift and hip hop...don't lie and say you don't too.

My love of reading started probably when I was three and it only made sense that I would start to create my own worlds since I was always getting lost in others'.

I like heroines who have to grow in order to become badasses, happy endings, and swoon-worthy, devoted, (and hot) male characters. If this sounds like you, I'm pretty sure we'll be friends.

I'm so glad to have you on my team...check out the links below for ways to hang out with me and more of my books you can read!

Visit my **Facebook** page to get updates.

Visit my Website.

Sign up for my newsletter to stay updated on new releases,

find out random facts about me, and get access to different points of view from my characters.

Books by C.R. Jane

www.crjanebooks.com

The Sounds of Us Contemporary Series (complete series)

Remember Us This Way

Remember You This Way

Remember Me This Way

Broken Hearts Academy Series: A Bully Romance (complete duet)

Heartbreak Prince

Heartbreak Lover

Ruining Dahlia (Contemporary Mafia Standalone)

Ruining Dahlia

Pretty Madness (Omegaverse Standalone)

Pretty Madness

The Fated Wings Series (Paranormal series)

First Impressions

Forgotten Specters

The Fallen One (a Fated Wings Novella)

Forbidden Queens

Frightful Beginnings (a Fated Wings Short Story)

Faded Realms

Faithless Dreams

Fabled Kingdoms

Forever Hearts

The Rock God (a Fated Wings Novella)

The Darkest Curse Series

Forget Me

Lost Passions

Hades Redemption Series

The Darkest Lover

The Darkest Kingdom

Monster & Me Duet Co-write with Mila Young

Monster's Temptation

Monster's Obsession

Academy of Souls Co-write with Mila Young (complete series)

School of Broken Souls

School of Broken Hearts

School of Broken Dreams

School of Broken Wings

Fallen World Series Co-write with Mila Young (complete series)

Bound

Broken

Betrayed

Belong

<u>**Thief of Hearts Co-write with Mila Young (complete series)**</u>

Darkest Destiny

Stolen Destiny

Broken Destiny

Sweet Destiny

<u>**Kingdom of Wolves Co-write with Mila Young**</u>

Wild Moon

Wild Heart

Wild Girl

Wild Love

Wild Soul

Wild Kiss

<u>**Stupid Boys Series Co-write with Rebecca Royce**</u>

Stupid Boys

Dumb Girl

Crazy Love

<u>**Breathe Me Duet Co-write with Ivy Fox (complete)**</u>

Breathe Me

Breathe You

Breathe Me Duet

<u>**Rich Demons of Darkwood Series Co-write with May Dawson**</u>

Make Me Lie

Make Me Beg

Make Me Wild

Make Me Burn

www.ingramcontent.com/pod-product-compliance
Lightning Source LLC
Chambersburg PA
CBHW051438150726
48000CB00005B/2147